The Eye watched Joanna.

She bought a new wig (auburn). She went to an oculist and had her eyes examined. She visited the animal veldt in Boca Raton. She went to the movies.

The Eye made a list of the movies she saw.

The Eye made a list of the magazines she bought.

The Eye made a list of her killings.

Seven of them that he was sure of. Four husbands. . . .

THE EYE OF
THE BEHOLDER

Marc Behm

BALLANTINE BOOKS • NEW YORK

A Ballantine Book
Published by The Ballantine Publishing Group
Copyright © 1981 by Marc Behm

All rights reserved under International and Pan-American Copyright Conventions. Published in the United States by The Ballantine Publishing Group, a division of Random House, Inc., New York, and simultaneously in Canada by Random House of Canada Limited, Toronto.

www.randomhouse.com/BB/

Library of Congress Catalog Card Number: 99-91350

ISBN 0-345-42799-8

Manufactured in the United States of America

First Ballantine Books Edition: December 1999

10 9 8 7 6 5 4 3 2 1

One

The Eye's desk was in a corner by the window. Its single drawer contained his sewing kit, his razor, his pens and pencils, his .45, two clips of cartridges, a paperback of crossword puzzles, his passport, a tube of glue, a tiny unopened bottle of Old Smuggler scotch, and a photo of his daughter.

The window overlooked a parking lot two floors below. There were eleven other desks in the office. It was nine thirty.

He was sewing a button on his jacket and watching the lot, where an old guy in overalls was rifling a yellow Toyota. The bastard seemed to have keys fitting all the cars and had already hit a Monza V8, a Citroën DS, and a Mustang II. He took a carton of cigarettes out of the yellow Toyota now, closed and relocked the door. Nobody could see him from the street because he was crawling on his hands and knees. He scampered over to a Jag XJ6C.

The Eye dropped the sewing kit into the drawer, pulled on his jacket, picked up the phone, and called the basement. A few minutes later three thugs from the guards' squad closed in on the old thief. They took his booty and the keys away from him, dumped a bucket of water over his head, and threw him out of the lot.

It was ten o'clock.

The Eye did the last four crosswords in the paperback, finishing the book. He tossed it into the wastepaper basket.

At ten thirty he borrowed *Le Figaro* from the girl sitting

1

at desk eight, read the headlines, the *Carnet du jour*, the
Vincennes racing results, and the *Programmes radiotélé-
vision*. He tried to do the French *mots croisés* but gave it up.

The young swinger at desk nine passed him *Playboy*,
and he looked at the nudes. All the girls were lying askew,
playing with themselves slyly. *"MISS AUGUST, far-out
Peg Magee (left), is turned on by Arab movies, skin diving, Mahler, and zoology."* *"MISS DECEMBER, demure
Hope Korngold (right), admits her erotic fantasies often
involve subways, buses, and ferryboats. All aboard!"*

He watched the parking lot again for a while. Then, at
eleven thirty, he took the photo out of the drawer and studied it. He usually did this for a half-hour or so every morning he was in the office.

It was a group shot of fifteen little girls sitting at tables
in a classroom. His wife sent it to him in sixty-one, in a
letter postmarked Washington, D.C. *"Here's your fucking
daughter, asshole! I bet you don't even recognize her, you
prick! P.S. Fuck you!"*

It was true—he had no idea which of the children was
Maggie. He'd flown to Washington and spent two months
looking for them, but there had been no trace of them
there. Watchmen bureaus all over the country tried for ten
years to locate them, then had just put the file away in the
dead archives.

He set the photo against the telephone on the desk,
leaned back in his chair, and crossed his arms.

Fifteen little girls with camera-shy faces. Seven or eight
or nine years old. One of them was his daughter. She
would be twenty-four years old this July.

His favorite for a long time had been the uncombed
moppet in the white sweater sitting under a crucifix hanging on the wall. She was holding an apple and scowling.
Then he'd switched to the blonde with the ponytail sitting
by the blackboard at the opposite side of the room. She was
biting a pencil. On the board was neatly chalked the beginning of Psalm 23: *"The Lord is my shepherd, I. . . ."*
Then, for years, his choice had lingered on the pale narrow
visage with the bangs in the last row. Her hands were
tightly clasped and she looked terrified. Then the girl next
to her had attracted his fancy. She wore glasses and was
grinning. . . .

But he no longer had any preferences. He knew them all by heart now and loved every one of them.

The classroom was the most familiar decor of his life: three walls, crucifix, tables, blackboard, the psalm, the apple. And the fifteen lovely faces, like infantile mug shots, the myriad of gazing eyes . . . and in the far corner a door through which he knew he would one day enter and call her name. And out of the multitude would rise his lost child.

He was absolutely certain of this.

He stared through the window. The old man in the overalls was back in the parking lot, looting the glove compartment of a Thunderbird.

The telephone rang. It was Miss Dome, Baker's secretary, summoning him upstairs.

It was noon.

Watchmen, Inc., filled two basement levels and the second, third, and fourth floors of the Carlyle Tower. Baker's office was in the northeastern corner of the fourth floor, an enormous salon with two Van Goghs, three Picassos, and a Braque covering one entire wall.

Baker was only twenty-nine years old. He had inherited the agency from his father a year ago. The old-timers downstairs ran the business, but he always handled what he called "the thousand-dollars-a-day clients" himself.

Two of them, an elderly man and woman, both in tweeds, were sitting in Hepplewhite chairs facing the refectory desk. Baker introduced them to the Eye: Mr. and Mrs. Hugo.

The Eye knew the name. Hugo shoe stores. Old-fashioned "booteries" (*Founded in 1867*) on downtown streets in all the big cities. He remained standing and tried to anticipate the squeal. A family problem, surely. A son or a daughter straying off the beaten track.

He was right.

Baker struck a pose, looking grave and professional. "Mr. and Mrs. Hugo have a son," he announced. "Paul. He graduated from college recently and is unemployed for the moment."

Mr. Hugo laughed nervously. "He's been unemployed for the last ten months!"

"He's made no effort at all to find a job," Mrs. Hugo said. "He's just loafing."

"He has a girl friend," Baker continued. "His parents want to find out something about her. They want to know just how deeply the boy is involved. You follow me?"

The Eye nodded. A college boy and a hustler. Dad and Ma desperate. A big retainer. He turned to Mr. Hugo. "What's the girl's name, sir?"

Mr. Hugo twitched. "We don't know. We've never met the young lady."

"She's been calling him up at the house," Mrs. Hugo whined. "That's how we found out about her."

Baker emerged from his chair, ending the session (he had a squash date at the Harvard Club at one). "Establishing her identity won't be any problem," he said. And he walked around the desk and stood staring at the front of the Eye's jacket. "They would like a preliminary report within twenty-four hours. Is that possible?"

"Yes." He fingered his buttonhole. The goddamned button was gone!

"Can we hear from you this time tomorrow?"

"Yes."

"That's all, then. Thank you."

The Eye bowed to Mr. and Mrs. Hugo and left the office. He wondered where the hell the button was. He found it out in the corridor, on the floor by the elevators.

On his last assignment he'd followed an embezzler named Moe Grunder to Cheyenne, Wyoming. (The guys downstairs called him "Grunder the Absconder.") He'd cornered the Eye in an alley one night and tried to brain him with a hammer. The Eye had shot him in the stomach. Watchmen, Inc., did not approve of killing suspects, and he'd been confined to his desk ever since. The Hugo job meant that the interdiction was lifted. The idea of escaping from the Tower and going out on the streets again elated him. He decided to skip lunch.

He took his sewing kit from his drawer and checked a Minolta camera out of the supply room. He went down to the second basement and asked the motor pool girl if he could have a car. She gave him the keys to the yellow Toyota.

He went out to the parking lot. The old thief in the overalls was still there, but scurried off when he saw the Eye coming.

It was a quarter to one. The sky was like greasy golden dishwater, the air tasted of hope and glee, the glittering windows of the Tower almost blinded him.

He climbed into the yellow Toyota and drove across the city.

The Hugos lived on Neatrour Avenue, in a house that looked like a gingerbread donjon.

He parked across the street. While sewing the button on his jacket he suddenly remembered the nudes in *Playboy*. Christ! Maybe one of them was Maggie! Miss August or Miss December. Why not? A superb nymph lounging naked on a page, caressing her thighs. Would he disapprove of such a thing? Probably not. In his fantasies he always pardoned her faults. Once he imagined finding her in a cellar with a rat pack of junkies. Her arms were festering with abscesses, and all her teeth were gone, but it never occurred to him to scold her. In another melodrama—he called it *Silent Night, Holy Night*—she was a whore who tried to pick him up in a skid row dive on New Year's Eve. She was wearing a mangy fur coat and looked positively ghastly. Tied to a string around her neck was a brass tiepin.

Where did you get this pin?

It's a souvenir. It belonged to my father. . . .

He took her to a sanatorium, and a week later she was cured and looked twenty years younger, glowing, green-eyed, clean, divine . . . and he finally recognized her. She was the moppet in the white sweater sitting under the crucifix in the classroom.

Daddy, I'm so ashamed.

Don't be silly.

Can you ever forgive me?

Balls!

He did the paper's crossword puzzle. Eight across, *Abundance of bread*. Nine letters. *Bakery. Bake shop.* No. *Affluence*. This was going to be an easy one. The Hugo job was going to be easy, too. He'd have to fake it, make it last. He didn't want to go back to that fucking desk for at least two weeks. He was always at ease out in the city, in the streets, in the traffic, moving through the labyrinth like a ghost, watching the tide of crowds, peering into crevices, looking for secrets. . . . Eight down, *Rex's daughter*. Eight letters. *Antigone*.

One of his very favorite reruns was called *Madame Agamemnon*. Maggie was the widow of a Greek tycoon, Kosta Agamemnon, "the richest man in the world." She'd met him in Iraq or somewhere (she was a student, studying archaeology at the University of Antioch). After a whirlwind courtship, they'd eloped to Paris where he'd dropped dead in their bridal suite at the Ritz on their wedding night. He left her a fleet of tankers and several banks and railroads and private islands. She came back to America immediately after the funeral and went to the Carlyle Tower. Baker called the Eye up to his salon and introduced him to her.

This is Madame Agamemnon. She wants us to locate her father.

The Eye gaped at the client. She was an exquisite young woman, almost a child, dressed in *Vogue* black, wearing glasses. Her hair was tied in a ponytail, and she was eating an apple. Baker was obviously impressed.

She wants us to put our entire staff on the assignment. The matter is extremely urgent and the expense is of no importance whatsoever. You'll be in charge of the case. Don't bother about the paperwork. You'll make all your reports to Madame Agamemnon in person. (Aside) *God damn it! You need a shave!*

May I ask . . . what is Madame Agamemnon's first name?

What the hell difference does that make?

Is it—Margaret?

Madame Agamemnon stared at him, her splendid green eyes blazing with surprise. *Yes, it is! How in the world did you know that?*

Horseshit! He finished the crossword puzzle, and he threw the paper into the rear seat. *Madame Agamemnon* indeed! He'd been letting himself glide for too long. One of these days young Baker would put the finger on him, and they'd take the .45 away from him and offer him a job emptying ashtrays and polishing the doors of the elevators.

Not that he really gave a rat's ass. Where the fuck *was* Maggie, anyway?

At two o'clock Paul Hugo came out of the house.

He was in his early twenties, long-haired, skinny, wearing a suit and tie, smoking a cigar. He got into a Porsche and drove uptown.

The Eye followed him.

The traffic carried them along Lafayette Boulevard and through the underpass into Second Avenue. Paul found a parking space at the corner of South Chilton. The Eye rolled past him and squeezed snugly into a slot in front of the Globe Building. He walked back down Second, twenty paces behind Paul. They went into a drugstore. Paul ate a sandwich. The Eye had two milk shakes and a slice of pie. Then, one behind the other, they walked over to Broad Street. Paul stopped in the lobby of the Lincoln Theater and looked at the *King Kong* stills. He lit another cigar. He crossed the street and entered the Capital Bank. The Eye was almost abreast of him, but invisible, as unobtrusive as the dot of an *i* in a paragraph. A guard, glancing at him, saw only a gray smear in a dapper landscape of passing suits. Not one note jarred, nothing blared, he left no spoor in his wake. If it hadn't been for that motherfucking button—he glanced at it, expecting it to drop off his jacket with a clang and roll across the marble floor like a wagon wheel—he would have been perfectly neuter.

Paul withdrew eight nine ten eleven twelve—the Eye counted the bills from the other end of the counter—thirteen fourteen fifteen sixteen seventeen eighteen thousand dollars from his account. Christ Almighty! He put the money in an envelope, pocketed it, left. The Eye got to the door first, five paces ahead of him. Paul followed him along Broad Street, passed him, cut through the Plaza Arcade to South Clinton. He stopped before a Hugo shoe store (*Founded in 1867*). The window was filled with wooden sabots, the latest rage in footwear. The kids called them clodhoppers. Twenty dollars a pair. He stopped again farther on, in front of a poster at the entranceway of the Ciné Club. *Dracula's Daughter* (1936). He lit another cigar. The eighteen grand baffled the Eye. What the hell was he going to do with all that cash? *Frau im Mond*

(1928). *The Cat People* (1942). Paul walked on. Eighteen thousand dollars! The Eye kept his distance—there were bad vibes here, and his radar kept hitting a mysterious splotch out in the abyss. A fraction of a second before Grunder the Absconder had tried to pound him with the hammer, he'd jerked the .45 out of his belt, took one step backward, and pulled the trigger. At that precise instant Grunder appeared and the hammer missed him. He felt exactly the same unease now.

Paul sauntered to Second Avenue and climbed into the Porsche. The Eye started to run toward the Globe Building. He slowed down, strolled. He boarded the yellow Toyota just as the Porsche rolled past him. Bad vibes!

They drove across Independence Circle and swung into Constitution Boulevard, passing the glass façade of the Air Terminal. That's where he'd met his wife. She worked there in fifty-two. The year the hydrogen bomb went off. *Atoll H*, eight letters. *Eniwetok*. Maggie was born in fifty-three. The year Stalin died. They'd both disappeared in fifty-four. The year . . . The Porsche floated into an opening at a curb side on South Park. There was room for two. The Toyota swerved in neatly just behind it.

It was four o'clock.

Paul walked into the park. The Eye took the Minolta XK and fell in behind him. Ragged boys and girls were strewn across the lawn like litter, playing flutes and guitars. The Eye snapped a picture of them. They jeered at him. He took a picture of the fountain. Paul sat down on a bench and lit another cigar. The Eye took some pictures of the playground, swarming with children. He bought an ice cream cone from a vendor over by the pavilion. On one of the pathways a hurdy-gurdy was playing "In the Shade of the Old Apple Tree." He snapped a picture of a little girl with a balloon. Christ! How did God plot the destinies of all these kids? You! You over there—*you!* You shall compose nine symphonies. And you shall be a taxi driver and you a mailman and you a private eye. You a typist, you a secretary of state, you a fag, you an embezzler. You shall write *Coriolanus* and you shall die in the electric chair. In the basement of the Police Center on Fair Oaks Street there was a map of the city, as vast as a dance floor, covered with flashing lights. Green for rape, red for homicide, blue for stickups, yellow for accidents. Maybe there was a map in Heaven, too, an almighty plotting board keeping track of everyone.

Hey, what about that eye in the park? Do you read him?

Loud and clear, Lord.

What's he doing?

Eating an ice cream cone. Vanilla and chocolate.

Is he cool?

Negative, Sire. He's got a bad vibes problem.

Shake him up!

And the girl appeared.

She came down a lane toward the bench. In her twenties, wearing a beret and a dark raincoat, carrying a valise. Closer . . . closer . . . lithe, supple . . . closer . . . closer . . . fair, gray-blue-eyed . . . closer . . .

Paul turned and saw her. He threw his cigar away, got up, hurried to meet her.

The Eye took her picture.

The hurdy-gurdy was playing "Shine on Harvest Moon." They kissed. The Eye took another picture. There was a funny taste on his lips, brassy. He wiped his mouth on his sleeve. His vision blurred. He tried to take a third shot but couldn't see anything. He leaned against a tree, blinking and squinting. Jesus! The park was as dim as a void, and his fucking ears were ringing. He dropped the camera. He tried to spit, snorted and blew his nose. Was he bleeding? God, he had to take a monstrous fucking leak! Well, all right, go ahead—nobody could see him, it was too dark. He unzipped with dead icicle fingers and squirted all over his trousers and shoes. Fuck all! What was he doing? Where was the motherfucking Minolta? The ice cream must have been poisoned! His cock was shriveling up. It vanished inside him! It was gone! *Gone!*

Two little girls came across the grass and hovered before him. He smiled at them. One of them picked up the camera, handed it to him. He took it, gurgled. Three old crones sitting on a bench on the other side of the green were gazing at him like a trio of basilisks. He could see them at least. But they could see him too. People looking at him! Wow! That shit had to stop!

He peered up at the sky. The sun blazed down on him.

Good. He was okay. Just numb. Yeah. Sure. Fine. Huh? Mmmm? Cool . . . cool . . .

The two little girls were tossing a ball back and forth. The old crones were knitting. Great! Everything was groovy. Except that he was unzipped, exposing himself in broad daylight next to a fucking playground.

He walked along the pathway and found a hiding place. He zipped up. His pants were soggy. He slipped through the trees. Don't touch your cock! It's still there, you poor creep! Upheavals always affect the genitals. Now . . . now then . . . so . . .

He looked back.

The girl was still there.

Their backs were to him, thank God.

Paul was holding the valise, and she stood with her hands on her hips, swaying, slightly awry, whispering to him. Then she turned quickly and glanced at the Eye, or beyond him, at—what? The flute players on the lawn? The fountain? The pavilion?

They walked off.

He followed them.

They went to the City Hall, two blocks away. They got married.

Two

The Porsche soared out of town via Belle Plaine Avenue then took the Clarion Overpass to Liberty Road. It roared through Ada, then Delphos, then Xenia, then Cedarville. The yellow Toyota was half a mile behind it all the way.

In the Eye's Minolta XK were several photos of the marriage ceremony. And a close-up of the two names on the Hall register: Paul Hugo and Lucy Brentano.

The bride was fron New York. She lived on East Ninety-first Street. She worked at the Air France office on Fifth Avenue.

At nine o'clock they arrived in Camden Lake and checked into the Woodland Inn.

The Eye left them there and drove to a gas station on 68. In the john he pulled off his trousers and scrubbed them with a damp rag. He threw away his shorts and soaped his cock and thighs. Then he had dinner in a restaurant in Evanstown, devouring everything that was served: salad, soup, veal, rice, an omelet, another salad, toast, cheese, a dish of cherries, cake, coffee, another cake, a double brandy.

At an adjacent table a drunk and his girl friend were arguing about Africa. She threw a bowl of gravy at him and he almost hit her with a jar of mustard, splattering the wall behind her. Three waiters bounced them.

The Eye had a peach Melba. Then another double brandy. At eleven o'clock he drove back to the Woodland Inn.

He parked the Toyota in a copse on the edge of the road and entered the grounds via a side gate. A lamp post glowed in the garden, painting the edges of the night in amber. He moved past the pool and tennis court, descended a narrow winding flight of stone steps to the back of the premises.

The newlyweds had a cottage suite on the lakeshore. All the lights were on. Floating as noiselessly as a shadow, he approached a window.

The living room was empty. Lucy's purse was on the couch. Her dark raincoat hung over the back of a chair. Her shoes were on the floor. A bottle of Gaston de Lagrange cognac and a pack of Gitanes sat on the coffee table.

The bedroom was empty, too. A silver disc on a chain was hanging on the bathroom doorknob. The valise, a dress, a collant, a bra, the beret, were scattered on the bed. A transistor on the bureau.

He went into the backyard, peered through a rear win-

dow. Paul, wearing only a pair of shorts, was in the kitchenette, smoking a cigar, taking glasses out of a cupboard.
He found two large liqueur ponies and carried them out
into the living room.

The Eye drifted back to the bedroom window. Lucy
came out of the bathroom, wrapped in a towel, wearing a
bathing cap. She took the chain from the doorknob and
hung it around her neck. She was barefooted; her face was
shining.

"Lucy!"

"Just a second."

She sat down at the foot of the bed, pulled off the cap.
Her hair was short cropped, tawny, citrine. She took a wig
from the valise, donned it. Now she was chestnut.

"The door's locked!"

"Is it?"

"What're you doing, closing me out?"

"Sorry. Force of habit."

She got up, crossed the room, unlocked the door. The
Eye slipped to the living room window. Paul was pouring
two cognacs. Lucy walked over to the table, picked up the
pack of Gitanes, lit one. He handed her a pony. She took
it, sipped it. He pulled aside her towel, touched the disc.

"What's this? A goat?"

"Capricorn."

"You're a Capricorn?"

"December the twenty-fourth."

"Merry Christmas! I'm a Leo. August the fifth. And
here we are!" He toasted. "Summer and winter. Hot and
cold."

They drank. The Eye backed off into the blackness.
Hold it! Capricorn? His radar was trilling again. On the
marriage register it had been Date of birth March 22, '54.

"Can I have some ice?" Lucy asked.

He came up to the window again. Paul set his pony on
the table and went into the kitchenette. Lucy walked over
to the couch, took a vial from her purse, uncapped it, carried it to the table, emptied it into his glass.

She stuffed the vial into the pack of Gitanes, sat down,
and finished her own drink. Paul came out of the kitchen
with a cup of ice cubes. He set it on the arm of her chair.

"I'm going to jump into a shower, honey."

"Don't be too long."

"I won't be a second." He picked up his pony and went into the bedroom.

It began to rain.

She uncorked the bottle, lifted it to her lips, took a long swig, then lit another cigarette. She rose, carried the cup of cubes out into the kitchenette.

The Eye turned up the collar of his jacket. A glint of lightning illuminated him. He cowered, moved along the wall to the bedroom window. Paul was in the bathroom, swallowing his cognac. He set the pony on a shelf, pulled off his shorts, turned on the shower, and, whistling, stepped under the spray.

The Eye was drenched. He took out his handkerchief, wiped his face. What was in the goddamned booze anyway? Chloral hydrate? An aphrodisiac? Cyanide? Balls! Capricorn. Maggie was a Cancer. The crab. His feet were soaked.

Lucy came into the room. She went to the bureau, switched on the transistor. A mezzo-soprano crooned.

> *Laisse-moi prendre ta main,*
> *Et te montrer le chemin,*
> *Comme dans la sombre allée*
> *Qui conduit à la vallée.*

Samson et Dalila. X across, *French composer with dash.* Ten letters. *Saint-Saëns.* She was going to kill him.

> *Tu gravissais les montagnes*
> *Pour arriver jusqu'à moi*
> *Et je fuyais mes compagnes*
> *Pour être seule avec toi.*

She leaned against the wall and smoked her cigarette. The Eye stared at her. She was going to kill him. Her hips moved in a contortion so exquisitely gracious that his throat choked with tenderness. The towel slipped from her body and she stood there, naked except for the chain and disc. She was going to kill him. He was absolutely certain of it.

Pour assouvir ma vengeance
Je t'arrachai ton secret . . .

Paul crawled out of the shower on his hands and knees.
He rolled over on the floor and squealed loudly.

Lucy walked to the closet, opened it. His suitcoat was
hanging on the inside of the door. She reached into the side
pocket, pulled out the envelope. She went to the bed and
shook the eighteen thousand dollars into her valise.

She turned off the shower, the radio, and all the lights.

The Eye wiped his ringing ears with his handkerchief.

He threw back his head and let the rain splash down on
his face.

Lucy reappeared at the back of the cottage, wearing a
raincoat, dragging the naked body out the door, through
the yard, and down the bank to a rowboat roped to a small
wharf. She hoisted him aboard, climbed in after him. She
cast off, lifted the oars into the locks, rowed away into the
rainy darkness.

The Eye sat down on the ground under a tree and
waited for her. Mud. He was sticky with mud. A sign on
the wharf warned:

> Don't swim too far from the shore
> Or you will drown and swim no more!
>   Pete Stone,
>   Camden County Sheriff

A few years ago there was a squeal the boys at Watchmen called "The Sinister Case of the Abominable Bathtub." A rare coin dealer named Nitzburg disappeared with
a sack of valuable Roman sesterces or something and Bill
Fleet, the missing persons expert—known on all the floors
as "Flatfleet"—spent four days looking for him. He finally
found him in his own bathroom, sitting in the tub, his left
side paralyzed. He'd been there for something like ninety
hours, unable to budge, gulping down mouthfuls of water
to stay alive. He survived. He sent Flatfleet a card every
Christmas. He—

Hold it. What did that have to do with this caper? Nothing. Some jobs were just simply more outlandish than oth-

ers. Well, anyway, *he* was covered. You could bet your ass on that! He'd tell them he went to his car to get his raincoat and when he got back to the fucking cottage they were gone. He'd say . . .

Lucy Brentano. What was her real name? What were her thoughts now, out there, all alone on the lake?

Hey! He could sneak into the bedroom and grab the eighteen grand and fade with it. He could say he lost their trail this afternoon and spent all night backtracking, trying to locate them. He could—

Shit.

He sat there, listening to the thunder.

She came back to the wharf. She roped the boat and walked up the bank, passing within five feet of him without seeing him.

He was invisible again, part of the landscape and the elements. Mud. A bog. The wind and the rain.

She entered the cottage, switched on a lamp, removed her raincoat, pulled on a pair of gloves. Nude, she took the money from the valise, dropped it on the pillow of the bed, went over to the closet and bundled all of Paul's clothing, then went into the bathroom and gathered up his toilet articles. She stuffed everything into the valise. The bottle of Gaston de Lagrange, too. And the transistor.

She was humming. The Eye, crouched at the window, trying to keep track of her movements, listened closely to the tune "La Paloma."

She lit a Gitane, washed the ponies, put them into the cupboard, then went through the entire cottage with a towel, wiping fingerprints from the sink taps, doorknobs, ashtrays, tabletops, the arms of chairs, the bureau, the closet door, the bathroom fixtures, the light switches.

Still wearing the gloves, she took a shower, then dressed and threw the gloves into the valise, picked up the eighteen thousand, and sat down on the bed. She leaned back on the pillow and, holding the money on her lap, went to sleep.

It stopped raining. The Eye remained where he was, afraid to move in the sudden stillness. He could see her feet and ankles, shining in a silvery haze of the lamplight. The rest of her was shrouded in shadows.

He filled his mind with pageants to ease his muscles. A

bullfight. A rodeo. Cars racing at Le Mans. A girl fencing with an Iroquois Indian. Maggie skiing. Paul wading out of the lake. A stage collapsing beneath a full symphony orchestra, all the musicians toppling in an insane avalanche of tuxedos and fiddles and oboes and cellos and bassoons. Insane indeed. Man, they'd catch her within twenty-four hours!

They?

Yes, they. The gentlemen down at Homicide.

What about them? Homicide? What homicide?

The bridegroom floating out there in the lake, man!

Suppose they don't find him for a while? A week, two weeks, a month? Or for that matter, never?

Never? (Aside) *He's right, by God! They'll never find him if they don't look for him!*

What does that mean, Daddy?

Huh?

She woke at five o'clock. She rose from the bed, picked up the valise, went into the living room. She put the money in her purse, put on her shoes and raincoat, went outside, and tossed the valise into the Porsche.

The Eye ran across the bank and up the stone steps. He raced across the garden to the side gate, tried to open it. It was locked. Sonofabitch! He climbed over it, sprinted down the road to the yellow Toyota. He jumped into it, started the motor.

The sun came up.

The Porsche stopped in the middle of the Camden Bridge. Lucy stepped out of it, threw the valise into the river and then her wig. She took another wig from her purse, pulled it on. Now she was a redhead.

She got back into the car and drove off.

The Toyota was half a mile behind her.

She parked the Porsche on Neatrour Avenue, a half-block from the Hugo's gingerbread donjon, and walked to Lambert Crescent.

The Eye followed her on foot.

The doorman at the Hotel Concorde knew her.

"Good morning, Miss Granger."

"Good morning."

She went into the lobby, took her key from the desk, and

stood with her hands on her hips, waiting for the elevator to come down.

The Eye sank into an armchair in the lounge. The house dick, a clod named Voragine, recognized him and came over, grimacing sourly.

"What's the matter with you?"

"Hello, Voragine."

"You look putrid."

"I've been up all night. Who's that?"

"Who?"

"The redhead there at the elevator."

"Name's Granger. Why?"

"Very nice."

"Eve Granger. From Frisco. She's a model."

"Very nice."

"You onto her?"

"No, no. Just looking. I'm onto something else."

"So what can I do for you?"

"Do you have a Baptist clergyman named Rathbone living here?"

"Rathbone?"

"The Reverend Jacob Rathbone."

"I don't think so. Stay put. I'll check the book."

He ambled over to the desk. The elevator door closed behind Miss Eve Granger.

He drove to the Carlyle Tower and left the yellow Toyota in the lot. He went down into the basement gym, showered and shaved. Lucy Brentano. Eve Granger. Fuck it! He kept a complete change of clothing in his locker. He put on a clean shirt, a new tie, another suit, fresh socks. He looked into a mirror and saw himself on the front page of a tabloid.

"DETECTIVE" HELD AS ACCESSORY! The role of Watchmen, Inc., in this tragic affair still has not been fully clarified. Why, for instance, was a private investigator (above) following the victim on the day of the murder? And how many interested parties were there out on Camden Lake the night Paul Hugo met his death?

Shit!

At nine o'clock he was in Baker's salon telling lies.

"Paul Hugo caught a plane to Montreal."

"Montreal?" Baker gawked. "When?"

"Eleven thirty last night. Air Canada Flight 586."

"With the girl?"

"No, all alone."

"God damn!"

"He withdrew eighteen thousand dollars from his bank account yesterday afternoon at three forty-five."

"What's he doing in Montreal with eighteen thousand dollars?"

"No idea."

"Well, find out! Get your ass up there right away!"

"Where?"

"To Canada!"

"What about the girl! We still don't know who she is."

"Drop her! Cover the kid. Christ, if we lose him, his parents'll flip all over me."

"Right."

He went downstairs to his desk, opened the drawer, pocketed his passport, the .45 and clips, and the classroom photo. He decided not to take his razor—he'd buy a new one. He left the office.

He never returned.

At twelve he was back in the lobby of the Hotel Concorde. Voragine came lumbering up to him, his dolt's face squeezed with annoyance.

"Now what? I don't like you comin' in here all the time sittin' in the chairs. Y'know?"

"I'm sorry to bother you, Voragine, but listen." He lowered his voice. "The Reverend Jacob Rathbone is probably using another name. Do you have anybody here with the same initials?"

"Same what?"

"The same initials. J.R."

"Could be. I'll check." He went to the desk.

Eve Granger came out of the elevator. She smiled at him as she dropped her key in the font. "Hello, Mr. Voragine."

"Hi, Miss Granger!"

She went out to the street. The Eye followed her. She crossed Lambert Crescent, turned into Seymour Street.

It wasn't the same girl he shadowed yesterday. Lucy Brentano had been grave and remote, fair and Saxon, a damsel in a Dresden tapestry, sitting on a rampart, reading the Venerable Bede. Eve Granger was bold and assured, vermilion and Celtic, doelike, bounding over highland brooks. She walked with long, agile strides and seemed to be always about to burst into laughter.

But both girls smoked Gitanes, wore the same silver disc on their throats. And as Eve stood window-shopping at Darcy's, her hands rose to her hips.

She was all in tan today—jacket, sweater, skirt—and wore ankle boots and carried a sack as huge as a mailbag. She—

She turned abruptly and looked over her shoulder.

The Eye passed her invisibly, lost in the vortex of pedestrians. But no . . . she wasn't looking at him. Something across the street had attracted her attention. He glanced at the opposite pavement. There was no one there. Only the crowd.

She bought a newspaper at a kiosk and two pears in a grocery store on Front Street, then went up to Bell Square and sat down on a bench.

The Eye pulled out the Minolta and snapped a picture of her munching a pear and reading the paper. She took a pencil from her pocket, marked a column.

He snapped four more shots of her.

She set the paper aside, finished the pear, got up, walked into South Clinton.

He went over to the bench and picked up the paper. It was folded open at the Horoscope section. The Capricorn box was encircled.

> Dec 22–Jan 20. This week there
> will be good days and bad days,
> laughter and tears, joy and
> heartache. Luck is still with you,
> take advantage of it. If you're
> planning to travel, now is the time.
> You have a secret admirer. Be
> circumspect.

So she and Lucy had the same sign, too.

She went into Stern's. In the luggage department she bought a small overnight case, then went upstairs to the Femme Chic floor and examined a rack of dresses. She selected a very simple, very expensive dark blue frock and took it into the dressing room and tried it on.

A floorwalker spotted the Eye and closed in on him.

"Can I help you, sir?"

"I'm supposed to meet my daughter here. We're going to buy an evening gown. But I can't find her."

"Do you want me to have her name called on the loudspeaker?"

"God, no! That would only embarrass her. Thanks anyway. I'll just stroll around."

She came out of the dressing room wearing the blue frock. A salesgirl wrapped up the tan outfit and put it in the overnight case.

Her next stop was the Footwear Shop, where she bought a pair of Italian shoes. Wearing them, carrying her boots in the case, she went downstairs to the ladies' room.

When she emerged she was a brunette!

And at two o'clock she met her next victim.

Three

His name was Brice.

She went into the parking lot of St. John's Hospital and stood waiting for him beside his car—a white Triumph in a private slot marked Reserved for Dr. James Brice.

The Eye panicked. They were certainly going to drive

somewhere and he had no wheels! There was a taxi stand on Windfall Lane, one lone cab at the curb. He flashed his fake badge at the driver, gave him a ten-dollar bill, told him to wait for him.

He went back to the lot. Eve was still alone, leaning against the Triumph, smoking a Gitane, one hand on her hip.

But she was no longer Eve. She'd changed again. Her exuberance and grins, her nervous energy and plentifulness were gone. She was languid now, somber, magic, Mediterranean—Cretan—no, farther East—Cyprus, the Euphrates, Parthia—a votaress in a blue smock, in a smoky temple, worshiping crocodiles. In a moment she would gaze into a basin of witches' slime and see him, standing behind her.

Instead, she ate the other pear.

Dr. Brice showed up at two sharp. They kissed. He was in his forties, handsome, trim, solid. He put her overnight case into the trunk, and they drove away.

The Eye ran down Windfall Lane and got into the taxi. He followed them to the Linker Bank and Trust Building. There was nowhere to park, so Eve drove the car around the block while Brice went inside. The Eye told the cabbie to stay with the Triumph and went after the doctor.

Brice withdrew twenty thousand dollars, which he put into a large billfold in his pocket. He went outside. The Triumph drove up, and he climbed in beside Eve. The taxi was just behind them. The Eye plunged into it, panting like a kettle. His chest was throbbing, his hands wet with sweat.

The traffic was murderous. The cabbie lost them on Maddox Drive, found them again on Lamont, lost them again on Riverside.

Then three trucks and a Jag wedged them into a jam and they stopped dead. Horns blared. A Doberman poked its python head out of the window of the Jag and bayed.

The Eye sprang to the sidewalk and ran up Riverside. A thousand cars were packed in the street. He turned down Gibbon, trotted into the Circle—stopped. Where the fuck was he going! He ran back to the cab. It was still there, squashed between the trucks and the Jag. He flopped into it. The Doberman barked at him. The jam broke, the traffic flowed on.

They drove into Frederick Avenue, passed the chapel on Woodlawn.

"They gave us the slip," the cabbie said.

"Yeah."

"Where'bouts now?"

"Keep going."

"Which way?"

"Straight ahead. No. Hold it! Stop here!" He gave him another five, just for luck, and walked back down Frederick to Woodlawn.

Why not? Flatfleet, the missing persons connoisseur, was always saying, "What's the pattern? Look for the pattern!" Well, this was a fucking pattern, wasn't it? The bank, the wig, Brice. And a motherfucking chapel!

He went up a pathway to the back of the chapel. The Triumph was there, in the rear parking area.

He went into the vestry and tiptoed into the nave. He sat down wearily in the last pew.

Eve and Dr. Brice were standing at the altar, getting married.

Her new name was Josephine Brunswick.

There were a dozen people present, all smartly dressed mod swingers in their twenties and thirties, smelling of green. Three pro photographers sat uninvited in a side pew, so—as usual—no one paid any attention to the Eye, slouched amongst them, holding the Minolta.

Lucy Brentano. Eve Granger. Mrs. Paul Hugo. Josephine Brunswick. Mrs. James Brice.

Who was she?

She turned slightly, glancing over her shoulder, looking at—what?

God Almighty! She was unutterably lovely. Her beauty stung him. He sat there, her scorpion's caress paralyzing him with rapture, her venom warming his blood. Who on earth was this girl? She had gray-blue-green eyes. She wore a goat on a chain around her neck. She often stood with her hands on her hips. She ate pears. She smoked Gitanes. She believed in the stars. And she was born on the twenty-fourth of December.

Capricorn. The Winter Symbol.

She killed a man last night and robbed him of eighteen thousand dollars. She was going to kill again tonight for twenty thousand.

He slid to his knees and prayed fervidly. *O Lord, don't take her away from me! Don't leave me all alone again, braying in the dark, like a wounded donkey!*

"I do," said Josephine Brunswick.

After the ceremony, the bride and groom, accompanied by the swarm of guests, went out on the front steps and posed for pictures. She'll never get away with this one. The Eye stood with the three photographers for a moment, taking a few shots. Then he ran to the back of the chapel and dashed like a madman from one parked car to another.

He found a brand new unlocked orange Honda Accord with the keys in the ignition. He sprang behind the wheel and drove out to Woodlawn Street.

He backed into the driveway of an empty house, stopped behind a hedge. It would be two or three hours before the hot car call went out to the cruisers. That would be time enough to fuck all.

Twenty minutes later the Triumph passed, heading south. He followed it.

They drove along Cooper Avenue and all the way down Jefferson Boulevard, past the University and the Country Club. At Stuyvesant they broke out into the open wilderness and Richland, Ormo, and Hayward flew by. They stopped at Fort Vale. Dr. Brice bought a carton of cigarettes; Josephine bought a toothbrush and a bottle of Gaston de Lagrange; the Eye bought a paperback of crossword puzzles.

The hot car squeal was circulating by now, but there were no patrols in sight. They drove on and on. At ten o'clock the Triumph pulled into the parking lot of The Cat's Pajamas, a roadhouse near St. Vincent.

A combo was playing. A girl in a see-through sari was

singing. Air Force officers from the nearby base were dancing with girls wearing awninglike dresses.

The bride and groom drank champagne and ate *cailles du Liban*. The Eye ordered a fifteen-dollar meal and devoured every calorie of it. While he was eating he did the first five crosswords in the book.

The room was a thick quicksand mire of well-being. Silver glittered on snowy tablecloths. Eagles flashed on natty uniforms. Jewels and women's eyes glimmered in the cloying dimness like harbor lights.

"This party's getting dirty!" a drunken Colonel shouted. "Give me back my pants!"

Everybody laughed. The Eye finished the fifth puzzle. Eleven down, *Blindfold*. Eight letters. *Hoodwink*.

He pulled the classroom photo out of his pocket and set it against the lamp. He invited the little girls to join him for dessert.

He had taken Maggie's phantom with him to so many places! To plays and concerts, to baseball games and racetracks and fencing matches. Wherever he went, she came along. And now they were eating ice cream together in an officers' dive in the middle of nowhere.

The fifteen little faces stared at him, making his heart ache. They were all gone now, claimed by others. Maggie, too. It wasn't fair. The game was rigged. God's plotting-board map was a rat trap; it lured wayfarers into no-man's-land and slaughtered them with time and loss.

Josephine dropped a spoon. Brice took her hand and kissed her fingers. She looked over her shoulder.

The combo was playing "La Paloma."

They got up and moved to the dance floor. The Eye sat back in his chair, folded his arms, watched them. They danced past his table.

She stood swaying just in front of him, her eyes closed. He'd never been this close to her before. Her left hand, on Brice's shoulder, pointed at him. The index was deformed, bent like a hook. Her eye paint in the half-light gave her face a mask's eeriness. Tiny pearls clung to her earlobes. Her flesh expelled the darkness, illuminating it, clothing her in a halo of incandescence.

Brice was aware of his scrutiny. He frowned, danced her away from the table.

Ten minutes later they left.

The Triumph turned off the highway and climbed a dirt road through a woods. A rustic sign with an arrow pointed into the trees—The Birdcage.

The Eye left the Accord in a glen and went up the hill on foot. In a clearing on the summit was a lodge with glass walls.

Brice was in the largest room, tossing lighted matches into a gigantic fireplace. Josephine was in one of the wings, pulling off her blue frock.

"Jim!"

"Ho?"

"Aren't there any curtains?"

"Any what?" Flames blazed in the fireplace.

"Curtains! On the windows!"

"What for? If anybody comes all the way up here just to peek, he deserves an eyeful!"

True enough!

Brice was in the other wing now, undressing, getting into a judo outfit. He combed his hair. Then he put a Vivaldi record on a Kenwood. The glass rooms and surrounding woods quivered with music.

Josephine opened the bottle of Gaston and poured a stiff drink.

The Eye went up on the porch and sat down on the railing. Brice came back into the main room, passing in front of him like a kung fu hero in Cinerama. "Do you like Vavaldi?" She didn't answer. "Jo!"

"What?"

"Do you like Vavaldi?"

"It's Vivaldi, Jim. Sure. He's peachy." She took off her bra and her stockings.

"What time do you want to leave tomorrow?"

"I don't care." She held up her crooked left finger, rubbed it with her right thumb. "There's no hurry."

"No. But it's a long drive. I feel like a beer. And we have to be in Miami by Friday."

He lit a cigarette. The Eye could see the pack. Larks. There was a steel bar in the corner of the room. He stepped behind it, lifted a lid, plucked out a can of beer.

He changed his mind. He took a bottle down from a shelf. The Eye could see its yellow label. Kahlúa.

He could see the goat disc, too, hanging on Josephine's naked breasts. She took her tan jacket from the overnight case, pulled it on.

Brice poured a drink. He was jittery. The Eye was certain they'd never been to bed together.

"Jim, these fucking windows make me nervous."

"You'll get used to it."

She turned out a lamp and disappeared. The Eye swung his legs over the railing and rolled off the porch into a pouch of darkness.

She came out of the house and stood beside him. She sipped her cognac, gazed at the woods. Brice joined her, pouring another Kahlúa.

"On nights like this I don't regret all the loot I spent building this pad."

"I'd like to live here."

"No way! It would mean a five-hour drive back and forth to town every day! Outta sight!"

"You could stay in town. I'd live here alone."

"Alone?" This took him aback totally. "What do you mean? You'd go bananas staying out here all by yourself. What would you do for kicks?" He was as cool as his vocabulary.

"Solitude," Josephine said. "Solitude and peace. What better kicks are there?"

"What would you *do?*" He set the bottle on the railing, a foot from the Eye's elbow. "I mean, like what would you do?"

"I'd listen to the wind and walk in the woods." She moved over to the opposite side of the porch. He followed her. "And lie in the sun all day."

"And at night?" He put his hands under her jacket.

"I'd go to bed and make love to myself." She leaned away from him. "Slowly and blissfully, as if I were sleeping with a friend . . . a dear friend . . ."

"Eh?" He was shocked. "What kind of nonsense is that? Masturbation is . . . lonely."

She laughed. "Where did you read that? In *Playboy*?"

He laughed, too, ashamed of his moribund reaction. He hoped she hadn't noticed. "Okay!" He was master of his swinging pad again, with a swinging chick in his arms, a tall, tanned, supple, mysteriously smiling centerfold chick wearing only a jacket, baby-doll-like, over her *in* thighs. In fact she was his wife. "Right you are, Mrs. Brice!" He was on his swinging honeymoon, with a swinging bride in his swinging Birdcage. "Right on! So just pretend I'm *you*!"

He dropped to his knees and kissed her stomach. Then his head was under the jacket and his nose between her legs. "Yum! yum!"

Josephine sipped her cognac, ignoring him. Then she looked over her shoulder, straight into the Eye's hiding place.

"There's somebody there, Jim!" She pushed him aside. "He's watching us!"

Brice jumped up. "You gotta be kidding!"

"Over there," she pointed. "Look!"

"There's nobody there, Jo!"

"Yes, there is!"

He went into the lodge and flicked on a switch. The Eye had dropped silently to the ground and somersaulted under the porch. A spotlight went on.

"You see?"

"I'm sorry," she laughed. "Weddings always make me paranoid."

"Come on inside, I'm freezing."

"I'm going to make a cup of tea. Do you mind, Jim?"

"Of course not!"

The light went out.

She was in the kitchen, drinking a cup of tea and smoking a Gitane. Brice was in the other room, squatting before the fireplace cowboy fashion, tossing twigs into the flames. A Bach record was playing.

The Eye paced around the clearing, his hands in his pockets. An owl cried in the woods. Three jets hissed by, coming into the base. Fighters. He remembered the stories in magazines he'd read faithfully every month when he was a boy. *G-8 and His Battle Aces. The Mark of the Vulture. Fangs of the Sky Leopard. Flight from the Grave.* Ed Billings lived around the block. He read *The Shadow.* Simonozitz, over on Second Street, bought *Doc Savage.* They'd pass them back and forth, like cranky scholars exchanging folios, arguing who was the greatest writer in America. Was it Maxwell Grant or Robert J. Hogan or—what was the other fellow's name? Roberts? He'd kept all the copies for years. His wife threw them away. Billings was in Washington. He got involved in the Watergate bit. Simonozitz was a dentist in Denver. His son was a TWA exec. Billings's ex-wife married an Italian count. She was in the movies now. He saw her in a picture last week, with Steve McQueen.

In the fishbowl kitchen Josephine pulled on a pair of gloves. She went to the buffet, pulled out a drawer, took a butcher knife, tapped its blade on the sink—ting! ting! ting! ting!

She walked over to the fuse box on the wall, jerked down the lever. All the lights died. Bach growled off.

"Jim!"

"It's all right, sweetie! Probably just a blown fuse!"

The Eye heard him walk into the kitchen, heard him scream. A pan banged to the floor. Another jet flew by. A chair skidded into the refrigerator.

Jo!"

The Eye walked over to the Triumph, kicked its tire.

Five . . . ten . . . fifteen minutes later the lights went on again. Josephine came into the main room. Her mouth was ajar, opening a deep gap in her face. The Eye watched her, appalled. She was going to scream! He waited, his hands on his ears. . . .

Christ! She was yawning!

He almost laughed. It was incredible! Jesus! That thing lying there in the kitchen wasn't really a corpse at all; it was simply an annoyance, a drunken boyfriend who had dropped in on her in the middle of the night and passed out on the floor. She'd let him sleep it off, and in the morning he'd apologize and leave. And in the meantime she would just tidy up a bit.

There was blood on her legs. She wiped it with a handkerchief.

The Bach concert continued.

She threw the handkerchief into the fireplace, removed her tan jacket, draped it neatly over a chair, opened a closet, took out a sheet.

She went back into the kitchen, wrapped Brice in the sheet, dragged him outside, rolled him off the rear porch and into the thickets.

The Eye retreated into the trees.

She found a shovel in the carport, dug a hole on the edge of the clearing, and buried him.

Now she was on her hands and knees, naked, scrubbing the kitchen floor. There was a smear of red on the refrigerator. She wiped it clean with a glove, soaped it, scoured it.

The Eye listened. She was whistling "La Paloma."

She went to the sink, washed the knife, dried it, put it back into the buffet drawer, poured a shot of Gaston, gulped it down, washed and dried the glass.

She took a clean towel from the pantry and went through the lodge, wiping away fingerprints. Then, still wearing her gloves, she took a bath. She dozed in the tub for a half-hour. The moon was high. Whippoorwills were singing all up and down the hillside. In her half-sleep she removed one glove and put her bare hand on her heart.

The Eye's throat was rank with thirst. He slipped into the kitchen and drank a glass of water. There was a spot of blood on the wall. He dabbed it with a rag. They were supposed to be going to Miami, so it would be days— probably weeks—before Brice was missed. Good enough. The grave was a risk, though. The freshly turned earth was a giveaway. And rats or foxes might uncover it. He took the shovel from the carport. He dug up the body, hauled it into the woods. He dug another hole in a patch of ferns. He reburied it, refilled the hole, came back to the clearing just as she climbed out of the tub. She shaved her legs with Brice's razor. That reminded him—he had to buy a new razor. She went into the other room and dropped the gloves into the fireplace.

He put the shovel back in the carport.

She dressed, putting on the boots and tan outfit. She packed the Italian shoes and her blue wedding frock in the overnight case. She took another long swig of cognac and then put the bottle in the case, too. She went into the bedroom again, pulled the billfold from the pocket of his coat, counted the money, stuffed the bills into her sack. She

found some more bills in his trouser pocket, at least two or
three hundred, and threw them into the sack. All his loose
change, too—quarters, nickels, dimes, everything. She
wiped the billfold with the edge of the bedspread, flipped it
to the floor under a chair. She lit a Gitane, picked up her
case and sack, came outside. She locked the door behind
her.

The Eye ran down the hill and got into the Accord. He
drove off toward St. Vincent. A few minutes later the
Porsche appeared behind him. He accelerated.

She followed him all the way to Fort Vale, then passed
him.

During the instant the two cars rolled abreast of each
other he glanced at her. She was looking straight ahead,
oblivious of him.

They got back to the city at seven thirty. She left the car
in a long-term parking garage, having changed wigs during
the trip. As she walked down Carter Street she was Eve
Granger again.

The Eye followed her, abandoning the Accord with vast
relief.

She went directly to the Hotel Concorde. The doorman
saluted her. "Morning, Miss Granger."

"Hi!"

She went into the lobby. Voragine waved to her. "What
d'you say, Miss Granger!"

"Good morning." She took her key and walked into an
elevator.

The Eye floated in, sat down in the lounge. Voragine
came over to him. "I saw Flatfleet in Scipio's last night,"
he said. "He told me you was in Montreal."

"I just got back."

"You catch that guy?"

"Not yet. I'm convinced he's still here."

"There ain't nobody at the hotel with the initials J.R."

"That doesn't mean anything What about R.J.?"

"R.J.?"

"You know, backwards. They often do that when they
change names. Just switch the initials around."

"Yeah, that's an idea. I'll take a look." He ambled away.

Eve Granger checked out at nine o'clock. She took a taxi to the air terminal. During the ride uptown she removed her wig.

She bought a one-way ticket to Chicago, paying for it in cash. Her name now was Dorothea Bishop.

Four

Without her wig and wearing no makeup, she looked much younger. Eighteen or nineteen. Her short-cropped hair was brushed down across her forehead and her eyes masked with dark glasses. She was in various shades of gray this morning, with black stockings, carrying a blue Lufthansa bag.

At the airport bookstore she bought a newspaper and a paperback, the Folger edition of *Hamlet*. She started toward the bar, then thought better of it, going into the lounge instead.

A cruising sailor tried his luck, asking her if she was, by any chance, Jennifer O'Neill. She didn't even hear him, sat down by a window, opened her paper to the horoscope page. Then she read *Hamlet* until her flight was announced.

She continued to read on the plane. She finished Act One and reread it, marking several passages with an orange felt pen.

Sitting across the aisle was a young man in a pink shirt. He leaned toward her.

"I beg your pardon," he said. There was no response.

"Excuse me—" She glanced at him. "Do you mind if I flirt with you?"

"Not at all," she said. "But wait until I finish this."

She read the end of Scene Five.

Rest, rest, perturbéd spirit.

She underlined it.

He got up, came across the aisle, and sat down beside her. A stewardess passed.

"A martini, please," he said and turned to Dorothea. "What will you have?" She didn't answer. He turned back to the stewardess. "Two martinis."

"No," Dorothea lowered her book. "A cognac." And she read on:

> O cursed spite
> That ever I was born to set it right!
> Nay, come, let's go together.

She put the book into her Lufthansa bag. She looked out the window at the infinity of blueness.

"It's not that I'm forward or brash or anything like that," the young man said, "but I always have to make the first move. It's defensive, you see. If a girl makes a pass at me, I'm immediately suspicious."

"Why?" She appraised him out of the corners of her eyes. Bronzed. About thirty. A Cardin suit. A striped velvet vest. A gold fountain pen. The pinkness of his shirt drenching everything.

"It's because of the business I'm in."

"What business are you in?"

"Oh, by the way, I'm Bing Argyle."

"Dorothea Bishop."

The stewardess brought them their drinks, and they toasted.

"Can I ask a very personal question, Dorothea?"

"Go ahead." She looked out at the sky again. She strained the muscles of her left hand, forcing the bent index to slide around the glass.

"What color are your eyes?" She pulled off her glasses,

faced him. He gasped. "Viridis, by God! I don't believe it! Pure viridis!"

"You mean green?"

"Don't be prosaic. They're Indian emeralds. Unalloyed spotless unblemished Rajasthan emeralds!"

"Hot dog!"

"I ought to know!" He glanced at the aisle, reached into his pocket, pulled out a small oblong velvet box. He snapped it open, smirking. It contained two large emeralds.

"Very impressive," she said.

"I'm not trying to impress you. If I was, I'd just give them to you. But they're not mine. I'm only a peddler."

"May I?" She took the box and held the gems against the porthole.

Puzzle Number Seven had the Eye completely stumped. Hints such as two down, *Leper King*, three across, *Captial in Czechoslovakia*, and one down, *Kraut Cat Five*, got him nowhere. He marked the page and went on to Number Eight.

Dorothea Bishop came up the aisle past his seat. A stewardess stopped her.

"Excuse me . . ." She wasn't at all sure of herself, but her eyes were as hard as stones. "You're not from Cleveland by any chance, are you?"

"No."

"Your name isn't Doris Fleming?"

"I'm afraid not."

"I'm sorry—it—the—" The stewardess stammered and tried to smile. "The resemblance is— A friend of mine was going with a—a girl who looks exactly like you. In Cleveland. A few years ago."

Dorothea put her hands on her hips. "I've never been to Cleveland."

"I could have sworn . . ."

"Everybody looks like somebody else." She walked on, entered the john.

Another stewardess came by the Eye's seat.

"It's her," the first girl whispered. "I'm sure of it."

"Who is she?" the other asked.

"She took a guy away from me once."

"Good riddance."

"They went off somewhere together, and that's the last anybody ever heard of him."

"Maybe he joined the Foreign Legion."

The two of them walked up the aisle.

The Eye got to his feet and moved aft. Doris Fleming! Christ! Sure! Why hadn't he thought of that before? Balls! He was forgetting every one of old Flatfleet's rule-of-thumb commandments. How many other bodies were there? How many wigs? How many names? The No Smoking sign went on. He could feel the deck tilting beneath his feet. And how many other witnesses could remember her and identify her? How long could she last?

The door opened, and Dorothea came out of the john, her lips tight with rage. She passed him without a glance.

At O'Hare she and Bing Argyle left the plane together. The stewardess was standing on the ramp, glaring at her. Dorothea smiled at her.

Bing was still trying smoothly to snare her, totally unaware of his own captivity. "Where are you staying, Dorothea?"

"I don't know yet. I've never been to Chicago before."

"What about the Ritz-Carlton? It's the only place, take my word for it."

"All right." She put her arm through his. "I'll take your word for it."

He beamed with conquest. They took a taxi together to East Pearson and checked into the Ritz-Carlton. She was given room 1214. The Eye managed to get into 1211, just across the hall from her. Bing was downstairs in 1109.

The Eye left his door ajar. He sat down on a cushion on the floor and watched the hallway. He returned to Puzzle Number Seven and tried to break it. *Leper King*, eight letters, *Kraut Cat Five*, seven letters, *Capital in Czechoslovakia*, four letters, and several other fucking twisters—*Ibis head*, *Arctic swordfish*, *Adrastea*—continued to thwart him.

Rain splashed on the window. A bellboy brought Dorothea a basket of pears. In the late afternoon she went out, wearing slacks and a turtleneck, overshoes, and a windbreaker, carrying an umbrella.

The Eye followed her.

They walked around the block twice. She gave a beggar woman fifty cents, then stood in the rain, gazing at the traffic. She walked down St. Clair Street, turned into East Huron, went all the way to the Lake, came back up the Drive to Pearson. She met the same beggar woman again on Seneca Street and gave her another fifty cents. She bought a *Trib* and leaned in a doorway, reading her horoscope. The Eye retrieved the paper when she threw it away.

> CAPRICORN. Health OK, if
> you don't overdo it. You need
> a rest, but who doesn't?
> Beryl is your color. Sat. is your
> day. AQUARIUS encounters
> are the best.

She ate another pear. On Michigan Avenue a black girl tried to pick her up.

She went back to the hotel at six.

At eight Bing Argyle, carrying an attaché case and a rose, wearing a scarlet Palazzi dinner jacket, knocked on the door of 1214. When he saw Dorothea, wearing a lime green evening gown, her hair wrapped in an olive silk band, he dropped to one knee in the corridor and imitated a trumpet.

"*Ta-ta-ta-taaa*! Crescendo! I swear it, you are—excuse my inadequacy—pretty!"

"What is your birthday?" she asked.

"February the seventeenth." He got to his feet. "Nineteen forty-five."

"Aquarius!"

"Yup. The water bearer. And the flower bearer." He gave her the rose. The door closed behind them.

Across the hall, the door of 1211 closed too.

The Eye went downstairs and waited for them. A half-hour later he followed them across the crowded lobby to the street.

"You'll love them," Bing was saying. "They're sweet people. They're Arabs."

"Arabs?"

"Egyptians, Iraqis, Syrians. They're so rich they don't

know what to do with all their shekels. One of them just—
get this—just bought three skyscrapers on North Michigan
Avenue. I love money, don't you?"

"Sure."

"But imagine John D. Rockefeller wearing a burnoose.
It's delirious!"

The party was in a high domino on North Boulevard, in
a penthouse overlooking the Shore Drive and Lincoln Park.
A sign on the door of the entryway read Jews Need Not
Apply.

Dorothea and Bing walked through several immense
ballrooms aswarm with Second City beautiful people enjoying a spree. Musicians in farmer duds were playing fiddles
and banjos, and two columns of guests were barn dancing.
One room was a Casbah *souk* filled with hucksters' stands
and booths and sweaty hirelings in turbans and djellabas
serving food and drink.

"Well met, Bing Argyle!" a voice called.

Bing led Dorothea over to the host, a round little man
who looked like a South American orchestra leader.

"Abdel baby!" Bing hugged him. "Shalom!"

"Bing, my dear! *Ravi de vous voir*. Who is this charming
girl?"

"Dorothea Bishop, Abdel Idfa. He's the Sheik of Kilo-
watt or something."

"Kuwait." Abdel kissed Dorothea's hand. "Welcome to
my party, fair maid. Oh, isn't she comely!"

"She's a skiksa, too," Bing said.

"Bing, do you have the merchandise?"

Bing held up the attaché case. "At your service!"

Abdel scowled at Dorothea. "Are you a virgin, child?"
he asked.

"That's none of your fucking business," she said.

Bing blushed and laughed, cackling. Abdel and Dorothea smiled at each other, both simmering with sudden
hate.

In the *souk* a Palestinian wearing sunglasses, a cream
suit, black and white shoes, a red shirt, and a purple neck-
tie, was standing in a bevy of student-looking girls, talking
about the Crusades.

"The Franks were far more imperialistic than the Romans or Jews," he said. "They annexed the entire country and called themselves the Counts of Tripoli and the Princes of Antioch and the Dukes of St. Jean d'Acre and whatnot. They tried to make serfs of all of Islam."

"My favorite person is Saladin," one of the girls put in.

"Yes," the Palestinian agreed. "*Salah-ed-Din*. Well, he put a stop to their freebooting."

"And who was the poor king with leprosy?" another girl asked. "He used to win all his battles lying in a basket, because he couldn't stand up."

"That would be Baudouin the Fourth," the Palestinian told her. "A figure of tragic repulsiveness."

The Eye pushed through the crowd. "What was his name?" he asked.

The Palestinian glared at him fiercely, his black glasses like holes. "Baudouin the Fourth," he said.

"He was king?"

"Yes. He called himself the King of Jérusalem."

"And he had leprosy?"

"He did. Why do you ask?"

The Eye walked off into the mob. *Baudouin!* Eight letters! That would unclog the whole fucking puzzle maybe! He went to one of the booths and ate a dish of ice cream.

Dorothea walked over to another booth and examined the array of bottles. She was alone. Bing was off somewhere with Abdel. She found a Rémy Martin and poured a drink. Lying on the end of the counter was a gold cigarette case. She picked it up and slid it into the bosom of her lime gown.

The Eye watched her from behind a nearby tent and followed her out of the room.

She joined the barn dance, spinning nimbly from partner to partner, skipping and hopping lightfootedly, grinning, flushed with pleasure.

The music ended.

She went out on the windy terrace.

She wiped her face with her arm and stood at the balustrade and gazed down at Lake Michigan. The North Shore traffic moved like a worm of gems around Lincoln Park. Her foot touched something. She bent over, picked up a Fourex pack. *Rolled in Foil Pink . . . natural skins . . . 'Non-Slip' XXXX . . .* She pitched it into the chasm.

She moved through a jungle of plants, her face raised, her nostrils sniffing the air. The darkness was scented with foliage and water. On a table before her was a scimitar in a rusty scabbard. She picked it up, drew out the blade. Her head turned, she looked over her shoulder. Through a window behind her she saw Abdel and Bing sitting at a table. Another man came into the room.

"Excuse me, sir. Mr. Iscari is here."

"Ah, good! Excuse me a second, Bing."

They left. Bing was alone. She rapped on the pane. He rose, opened the window. His jowls spread in surprise.

"Dorothea . . ."

He came out on the terrace and walked straight into the blade. It pierced his abdomen, traversed him.

She went into the room, picked up the emeralds, ran back across the terrace into the crowded penthouse. A TV comic was standing in a whirlwind of laughter, telling jokes. The crowd applauded. In the entryway coats and wraps were piled on chairs and sofas. She took a mink, slipped into it, went out to the elevator.

The Eye tugged Bing through the plants, rolled him into a corner of the terrace behind a row of pots. Abdel came out of the room.

"Bing? Where are you, my dear?"

The Eye clubbed him behind the ear with the edge of his hand, toppling him. He dragged him into the greenery, pushed the table in front of him.

The TV comic was firing joke after joke into the storm of laughter and applause. No one paid any attention to the Eye as he wandered across the room into the entryway.

The Elevator carried him down to the lobby. He ran out to North Boulevard.

She was a block away, walking down Astor Street toward East Burton.

He followed her.

She turned west, along Burton, then south down Dearborn, then west again to Clark, then south again down Clark all the way to Goethe Street.

They took two taxis back to the hotel.

It took her exactly seventeen minutes to change clothes, pack, pay her bill, and check out.

Two more taxis drove them to O'Hare. They caught a

late flight to New York. The name on her ticket was Annie Greene.

On the plane she emptied Marlboros out of the gold cigarette case and filled it with Gitanes. Then she read *Hamlet*.

The Eye worked on Puzzle Number Seven. *Leper King* was *Baudouin*. *Ibis head* had to be *Thoth*. *Arctic swordfish* was *Narwhal*. *Kraut Cat Five* was a German Mark V tank, a *Panther*.

But *Capital in Czechoslovakia* still confounded him. In fact, everything confounded him, the whole fucking bit!

But he refused to think about that.

He took the class photo from his pocket. Annie Greene finished Act Three. Scene Three.

My words fly up, my thoughts
   remain below;
Words without thoughts, never
   to heaven go.

She sat the book aside. The Eye studied the faces of the little girls. Annie held the two emeralds in her fist and rattled them like dice.

Then they both fell asleep.

The Eye dreamed he was walking down a long corridor. He thought he was back at the Ritz-Carlton. But no . . . he opened a door and saw blackboards, a crucifix, rows of empty desks. It was a school! He opened another door, calling his daughter's name. He found himself in a bare, damp chamber, standing before an old man with a rotting face, who sat on a throne, holding a map on his lap.

I have been plotting your course, he said.

Who are you? the Eye asked.

I am the King of Jerusalem.

And he held out his arms, showing him his leper's paws.

Five

A brief five lines appeared in the New York papers the
next day announcing the murder of Kent "Bing" Argyle.
According to the Chicago police report, his body was discovered in Lincoln Park at nine o'clock in the morning,
stabbed and robbed. Dorothea Bishop wasn't mentioned.
Neither was Abdel Idfa.

The Eye read the story, relieved. The Arabs were staying
away from it. They'd smuggled the body out of the penthouse and were now just going about their business, giving
away no leads whatsoever. Kismet!

So Annie Greene was safe.

But she was no longer Annie Greene. She was registered
at the Park Lane Hotel on Central Park South as Daphne
Henry (blond wig). She sold the two emeralds to a fence
on Bedford Avenue in Brooklyn. She'd had dealings with
him before; he thought she was a Hungarian refugee
named Marta Ozd (red wig). She put her money in a safe-
deposit box in a bank on Jerome Avenue in the Bronx
where she was known as Erica Leigh (platinum wig). She
spent most of her time in a girls' private club on East
Fifty-ninth Street. Her name here was Debra Yates (no
wig).

Lucy, Eve, Josephine, Dorothea, Annie, Daphne, Debra . . . he gave up trying to sort out her identities. All
the Minolta XK photos of her were spread about the floor
of his room at the Park Lane, just next door to her suite.
He sat staring at them miserly. The best of all was the very

first, the young woman he saw in the park at four o'clock one afternoon, walking along a lane of trees, coming into his life like Grace, smiting an unbeliever.

In another picture, snapped in the O'Hare waiting room, she stood with her hands on her hips, staring into the window of a boutique. The bent index of her left hand was curved against her waist, a pathetic asp curled in a nest.

He kissed it gently.

Pity seized him, holding him fast in a grip of agony. His eyes burned with tears. He bit his lip, swallowing a sob. It sank down into him, gulping in his throat and filling his lungs with electricity and fishhooks.

He looked at the wall.

She was there, less than five feet away from him, splashing in her bath. He could hear her whistling. He got up, crossed the room.

He touched the wall.

Then guilt and dismay lashed at him furiously.

Poor Maggie! He had betrayed her. Usually, his every third thought was for her, guiding her, phantomlike, past every pitfall and jeopardy his anguish could invent. Now she was an orphan, erring alone—where? While he worshiped this goddess bathing in the next room, who would protect his daughter—if only with a thought—from the daily vileness of growing up—from the back alleys, the vacant lots, the garbage dumps, the cellars, from the sex creeps in doorways with their cocks hanging out, from the street sharks, the subway freaks, the pushers and pimps, the muggers with ice picks and the junkies climbing across roofs like dacoits, from all the ghoul-people of the city wilderness?

His nails clawed at the wall and he whimpered like a dog in a kennel.

She and five or six other girls worked out in the club gym all morning, three days a week. Two of them were debs with nothing else to do. The others were actresses and models.

At noon they'd swim nude in the attic pool. One morning the Eye gave the janitor of the adjacent building ten dollars so he could watch them through a skylight. Later, in a cafeteria on First Avenue, he listened to two of them talking about her.

"I think she's a dyke. I bet she's making it with Ditty after we leave."

"No way. I touched her once in the water and there wasn't any turn-on."

"Those eyes of hers scare the shit out of me."

"I love her ass. It's just right."

"She looked at me the other day and I got dizzy."

"I wonder what she *does*."

"I had a cat with eyes like that. A real mean little beast."

"If I had her ass, I'd be making four grand a week."

"That mink she was wearing must have cost four grand."

"I asked her. She said she picked it up out West for practically nothing."

The next time he tried to spy on the swimmers the janitor wouldn't let him into the building.

"Get lost!" he said. "A guy came up there yesterday and I caught him jerkin' off! I'm not runnin' a massage parlor!"

Debra Yates was sitting naked on the edge of the pool, reading her horoscope.

> You are too impulsive. This is
> no time for heedless action.
> Do not solicit unnecessary
> complications. Have confidence
> in a steadfast friendship.

The other girls were diving and frolicking around her, eyeing the overhead skylight, trying to get a glimpse of any onlookers who might be up in the loft windows of the place next door, watching them. Whenever they were sure someone was there, they'd begin their orgy act, writhing on the poolside like bacchantes pretending to go down on one another, dancing lewdly on the diving board, daisy-chaining in the water, working themselves into a wanton frenzy.

Debra took no part in these antics. She would swim her twelve lengths (one under water), then eat a pear or read or just loll until she got cold, then leave.

She seldom gossiped, had no friends, rarely laughed.

Speculation about her ran wild. She was an ex-nun. She graduated from Vassar. She was the illegitimate daughter of the Shah of Iran and an Apache squaw. She was the highest paid call girl in Manhattan, specializing in anilingus, bestiality, S/M, scatophagy, est sex, and United Nations representatives. She made porn movies in LA. She was the WASP plaything of a Mafia don. She was a Martian. She was frigid.

Finally they all decided she was simply bizarre and let it go at that.

Ditty, the club's manageress, came over to her. "Come here, Debra, I want to show you something."

Debra got up and followed her around the pool to a front window. They looked down at Fifty-ninth Street. "Shit," Ditty said. "He's gone. He was standing over there in front of Charlie's joint."

A sudden chill blew goose pimples over Debra's nudity. "Who was?" She wrapped a towel around her shoulders.

"Listen." Ditty slipped her arm around her, taking advantage of their conspiracy to fondle her shoulder. "The other day—Friday—I was downstairs, out front, waiting for Romy. I wanted to see who was driving her car." Romy worked in the gym. She was Ditty's girl friend and was constantly involved in shady infidelities. "I thinks she's playing come-and-get-it with Liz. You know, the broad at Hunter College. Having a quick one every now and then on the side."

"And what happened, Ditty?"

"Well, I was very alert, otherwise I wouldn't've noticed. This guy walked by, see. Then he came back. Then he came back *again*. He passed four or five times. He was there when you left. He tailed you."

Debra huddled in the towel, her shoulders hunched, her hands crossed on her breasts. "Maybe it's just one of the creeps next door," she said.

"I don't think so, Debra. Like Monday he was here again. He had on a duffel coat. He drifted by, see, toward York Avenue. Then five minutes later there he was, crossing the street, coming from First. He was wearing a Harris Tweed jacket. Then back he comes, in a fucking raincoat! He's probably got a car parked somewhere and keeps changing his clothes. The dingdongs next door wouldn't go to all that trouble."

"Describe him."

"So-so. Medium. Average."

"That's not a description, Ditty!"

"How the fuck d'you describe men? They're amorphous. I'll show him to you when he comes by again."

But he didn't come by again. The Eye saw them standing together in the window and faded back to his car.

She came down First Avenue, entered an office building on the corner of East Fifty-seventh, and stood in the lobby watching everyone who came through the doorway behind her. Fifty people passed. She tried to memorize all the men.

She walked seven blocks to Fiftieth Street, turned west, crossed Second, Third, and Lexington. She went into St. Bartholomew's Church on Park Avenue, sitting in a rear pew to watch the door. Fifteen minutes passed. A man entered. He was in his late sixties, tubby, rosy, white-haired, wearing a double-breasted topcoat. He minced into a pew across the aisle, brushed the bench fussily with the tips of his fingers before sitting down.

He glanced at her furtively, blinking, his face jumping with tics. He pivoted toward her, unbuttoned his coat. Hanging between his thighs from a length of string tied around his waist was a large green cucumber. He shook his hips, flopping it at her. Then he jumped up and trotted out the door.

She sat there a moment longer, stifling a smile and giving him time to escape. She went out to Fiftieth, walked to Madison, turned north.

She entered a Hugo shoe store (*Founded in 1867*) on East Fifty-fifth. She stood in the front window, staring out at the sidewalk. She told the clerk she was waiting for a friend.

A thousand people passed—two thousand, three thousand. She saw only the men, an endless cavalcade of male profiles—noses, ears, chins, torsos, bellies, hats, warts, grimaces, moles, squints, glasses, cigars, pipes. . . .

She left. She bought two pears in a grocery on Fifty-sixth, ate one of them.

On Fifth Avenue she took a subway to Queensboro Plaza.

She ate the other pear, studying the faces of the passengers. A soldier. A Japanese. A boy in a baseball cap. A priest. A black. Another Japanese. Three men who looked like burglars, carrying bags of tools. Two deaf-mutes waving their fingers, emitting bird noises. A cop. A dozen others . . . all blank faced, featureless, as expressionless as closet walls.

She took three buses to Greenpoint, the Navy Yard and DeKalb Avenue. She ate a hamburger in a drugstore. She stopped once and looked over her shoulder, certain he was standing just behind her.

She went into the subway again on Pacific Street.

She spent all afternoon and half the night rolling up and down Brooklyn on the Fourth Avenue, West End, and Brighton Beach Lines. She changed cars every four or five stops. She went back and forth from Coney Island four times. She was sure she never saw the same face twice.

At one o'clock in the morning she checked into a grubby hotel on Kings Highway. She gave the night clerk ten dollars.

"I want you to write down the names of everyone who checks in after I do," she told him.

He sniggered at her. "What for?"

"For another ten when I leave tomorrow."

"That's an all-night job, lady," he smirked. "Better make it twenty."

She gave him an extra ten. She sat up all night in a clammy room, watching the street. At six o'clock she went down to the desk, and he handed her a copy of *Penthouse.* Scrawled on its cover were three names:

> Mr. & Mrs. Clark Gable
> Mr. Wm. O'Something
> Mr. Ed Dantes

She gave him his twenty dollars and sat in the cubbyhole lobby reading the *Penthouse,* waiting for them to check out.

O'Something came down at six-forty. He was as tall as a circus giant and carried three heavy valises. He drove away

in a car with Idaho license plates. Mr. and Mrs. Gable
were a hooker and her john, both Puerto Ricans. They left
at seven ten. Ed. Dantes was the Eye.

He saw her as he started down the stairs. He retreated
silently into the upper hallway and climbed out a window.
He jumped down into the backyard, ran across a lot into
the adjacent street.

She sat there until nine, watching the stairway. When
the day man arrived, she had him ring his room. There was
no answer.

She left.

He was on the platform of the Kings Highway station
when she took the train back to Manhattan, but she didn't
see him.

She returned to the Park Lane Hotel and took a bath.
Then she began again. She went to the club, and she and
Ditty watched East Fifty-ninth Street until after two.

Lunch in a Chinese restaurant on Third. A movie on
Forty-second Street. She crossed Central Park to West
Seventy-second, then walked down Columbus Avenue to
Broadway. She had dinner in a pizzeria near Grand Cen-
tral. A man in a beige suit and Hawaiian shirt sat at the
next table, ogling her, spoiling her meal.

She went to a bar on East Fifty-fourth and drank two
cognacs and read *Hamlet*. At midnight she telephoned the
Kings Highway hotel and asked the sniggering night clerk
if she could talk to Mr. Dantes.

"Who?"

"Mr. Dantes."

"Gone."

"Did he leave a forwarding address?"

"Are you the beautiful lady who give me the two twenties?"

She hung up. The man in the beige suit and Hawaiian
shirt came into the bar as she was leaving.

She drifted down Fifty to Forty-second Street, then up
Broadway to Seventh.

Two drunken marines swooped down on her out of nowhere. Whooping, they lifted her off her feet and whirled
her across the sidewalk, fighting over her playfully, maul-
ing her between them. She broke away from them, shoved

them aside. They wobbled off the curb into the gutter, and a swerving taxi hit one of them, sending him spinning into the crowd like a drunken dervish. Someone screamed.

She walked on slowly, not looking back.

She turned the next corner, stood in a doorway. The front of her dress was torn open, her necklace was broken, the disc was gone. She took her blond wig from her bag, pulled it on.

She pinned the dress, crossed Fifty-seventh Street. Ten minutes later she was in the deserted lobby of the Park Lane. The night man gave her her key.

"Good night, Miss Henry."

"Good night."

In her suite she removed the blond wig and sat down at her dressing table, catching her breath. Her dress was ruined. She donned a pair of gloves.

A key turned in the lock, the door opened. The man in the beige suit and Hawaiian shirt strolled into the room.

The Eye stood under a lamppost on Seventh Avenue, thinking about Puzzle Number Seven and watching the marines play with Daphne Henry.

Arctic swordfish, six letters down, had to be *Narwhal.* So *Adrastea* was *Nemesis.*

He saw the taxi coming.

But *Capital in Czechoslovakia,* four across, didn't make any sense at all. In fact, the whole bit was turning into a monumental pain in the ass!

He lunged forward, stumbled against one of them, shoved him off the curb. The marine lurched into the gutter and the taxi hit him, pulverizing him.

But the goddamned crosswords had been a perfect cover all these years, he had to admit that. They camouflaged everything.

Someone screamed.

Nobody—but nobody!—knew just how really nutty he was. They all thought—Baker and Flatfleet and the zombies sitting in the room with the eleven desks—they thought he was just eccentric. *Oh, him! He's harmless. A crossword puzzle freak. He's been like that ever since his wife left him. Spaced out.*

He followed Daphne over to Fifty-seventh Street.

It had started in Washington, D.C., the year he'd spent six months looking for Maggie. One night he'd woken up at three in the morning and found himself sitting out on the ledge of his hotel room, ten floors above the street. He'd crawled back into the room, opened a magazine, and spent the rest of the night doing a crossword.

And he'd been doing them ever since.

Then there had been that horror in the alley in Cheyenne. Jesus! In that last instant, just as the hammer was swinging, he'd looked at Grunder and seen his horns and his tail! And when the bullet hit him, he'd vomited flames.

Spaced out indeed! Wow!

That's why going back to the fucking office was impossible—for the time being, anyway. He couldn't hide behind himself forever. Sooner or later somebody was bound to catch on. And when that happened, they'd close in on him with butterfly nets and he'd end up gibbering out on the ledge forever.

He prayed: *Not now, Lord, not yet! Let me stay loose for just a little while longer.*

He needed a rest . . . a haven . . . peace . . . shelter. He needed *this. Her.* She was his appeasement, his rod and his staff in the valley of death. And he was hers.

He followed her into the Park Lane Hotel, just behind the man in the beige suit and Hawaiian shirt.

"Your name is Daphne Henry?"

"Yes."

"I'm Sergeant Sheen, NYPD."

"What can I do for you?"

"You dropped this." He showed her the silver disc.

"That's not mine."

"Yeah it is."

"Who gave you the key to my room?"

"Night guy downstairs. He says you're from Iola, Kansas."

"That's right."

"It's yours." He tossed the disc into the air, caught it as it fell. "Would you walk away from the scene of an accident in Iola, Kansas?" She was trapped against the table. He was standing before her, leaning forward, almost touching her. "Well, it's against the law in New York, too."

"How much?"

"What?"

"How much will it cost me?"

"Are you trying to bribe me, kid?"

"I just want to know how much the fine will be."

"Five hundred dollars," he grinned at her. "What's this stuff?" He pointed to a bottle on the table.

"Courvoisier."

"What's that?"

"Cognac." She removed her gloves, threw them on the sofa.

"Five hundred dollars and a shot of it."

"Help yourself." She eased past him, walked over to a tray of glasses on the commode. "Make it two." She handed him two ponies. "Where did you get that ugly shirt?"

He took off his jacket, hung it over the back of a chair. "Store on Third Avenue. Had a sale. I bought six of them." He was wearing a holster clipped to his hip. "What do you do for a living, Daphne?" He filled the two glasses.

"I'm a wigmaker." She took the wig and set it on the mantelpiece. "I'm in New York trying to sell some of them."

"Is that what you was doing roaming around the streets at one in the morning? Drumming up trade?"

"I was just sightseeing."

"Can you show me some identity?"

"Some what? Identity? Certainly."

"Your dress is ripped." He unclipped the holster, dropped it on the table.

"It doesn't matter. I have several dresses."

He drank his cognac, forcing it down in one gulp. "Wham," he said, then poured another. He gave her her pony. "Take it off."

"Driver's license?" She pulled off her dress. "Credit cards? What would you like?"

"You know what I'd like, babe." He walked across the room, unbuckling his belt. He lowered his trousers, sprawled in a chair. "You sure you got five hundred?"

"Yes."

"All right, then, I guess we can make us a deal." He pulled down his drawers. "Come here."

She swallowed a mouthful of cognac and moved to the
table. She set the glass aside, picked up the holster, opened
it.

"Don't touch that!" he shouted.

She turned and shot him in the face.

She went to the sofa, put on the gloves. She picked up
her dress, wiped the gun, then her pony. His glass was on
the floor. She rubbed it clean. She glanced around quickly.
There were no other prints anywhere, she always wore
gloves in the suite. She had already decided that her luggage would have to be sacrificed. Too bad. She pulled her
platinum wig from a valise, put it in her bag. She took her
silver disc from the pocket of his jacket.

She ran down the service stairs—ten floors—to the basement. She went through a dark, throbbing gallery, which
echoed with the thumping of machinery, like the hold of a
ship. A watchman was snoring on a cot in an alcove. She
tiptoed past him, unbolted and opened a door.

She walked up Central Park West to Seventy-second,
turned into the park. She climbed a steep knoll and sat
down under a tree.

She remained there until dawn, watching the woodland's
elf denizens come and go in the moonlight around her.
Three boys made love in the grass just in front of her. Two
others stripped and donned tutus, then disappeared, whistling, into a dark lane.

At five thirty she descended the hillside and took a subway on West Seventy-second to the Bronx. She rolled all
the way to the Dyre Avenue terminal, then came back to
180th Street. Then she went all the way to the 241st Street
terminal and came back to 149th. From there she went all
the way to Woodlawn and back.

She killed three hours this way.

At eight thirty she had breakfast in a coffee shop on
Tremont Avenue. At nine ten she put on the platinum wig
and went to the bank on Jerome Avenue. She emptied Erica Leigh's safe-deposit box. While waiting for a taxi to
show up she ducked into a store and bought a suitcase. She
took it with her, empty, to Kennedy Airport.

She bought a ticket to Los Angeles, using the name
Charlotte Vincent.

Six

She sat in the airport cocktail lounge, naked under her mink, rereading *Hamlet* and drinking a Gaston de Lagrange. With a red felt pen she underlined

> There's a divinity that
> shapes our ends. . . .

She was alone, except for a man sitting at a corner table.

"What time is it?" he asked. She didn't bother to answer.

"What time is it, please?"

There was a clock on the wall just above them. She pointed to it.

"I beg your pardon, could you tell me the time?"

"Ten forty."

"Thank you."

A few minutes later he knocked over his drink. A waiter came across the room and wiped up the mess.

"Sorry," the man said.

"That's okay. Another one?"

"Yes, please."

She stared at him, intrigued. He was in his fifties, lean, gray, calm. His hand groped around him. She looked down. Lying on the floor beneath his chair was a cane. She got to her feet, went to him, picked it up, placed it in his hand.

"Thank you."

She went back to her table, sat down. He pulled out a billfold, extracted a ten, fingered it sightlessly. The waiter brought him another drink.

"I'll pay now."

"Yessir. Five sixty." He took the ten. "This is a five, sir."

"Is it? My apologies." He fumbled in the billfold for more money. "I thought it was a ten."

She glared at the waiter, outraged. "It is a ten, you goddamned fink!"

He glared back at her. "Oh, yeah, so it is. My mistake." He walked off, boiling. The man chuckled.

"Waiters are always pulling that on me," he said. "Actually, I can tell the difference between a ten and a five."

"How?" she asked.

"I fold them differently."

"Very clever."

"Peace be with you," he toasted.

"Amen," she said. They drank together.

"What are you reading?"

"How do you know I'm reading?"

"I can hear you turning the pages."

"*Hamlet*."

"I have it on records," he said. "Burton, Barrymore, Gielgud, Evans, Leslie Howard—everybody. A dozen albums."

"I saw it with Richard Burton."

"I've never seen it," he said matter-of-factly. "Why are you reading *Hamlet*?"

"There's a line in it that fascinates me," she laughed. "It's like listening to your favorite song over and over again. It always takes you by surprise."

"What line?" he asked.

She turned the pages back to Act Two, Scene Two and read, " 'For murder, though it have no tongue, will speak with most miraculous organ.' "

The LA flight was announced.

"That's me," he said.

"Me too. Can I give you a hand?"

"I'd appreciate it. My name is Ralph Forbes."

"Charlotte Vincent."

The waiter watched them leave the lounge together. He turned to the barman. "Real cool," he grumbled. "She'll probably take him for everything he's got."

The Eye thought exactly the same thing.

* * *

As they walked through the ramp she glanced around at the other passengers.

"Looking for somebody?" Forbes asked.

"I thought maybe—a friend of mine might be here to see me off."

He touched her wrist. "Easy," he whispered.

She looked at him, startled. "What?"

"Your pulse," he said. "Beating much too fast. Beware of hypertension."

"I hate flying."

"I'll take care of you." He patted her arm. "Nothing can happen to you when you're with me."

She stared at him, dumbfounded.

They sat in the quietly humming serenity of the first-class cabin, forty thousand feet over Pennsylvania.

She watched his profile out of the corners of her eyes. He had a hooked nose and a chin like a stubborn *C*. There were shaving scars on his cheek.

He unzipped a flight bag and produced a bag of candy. "Have one of these. They're supposed to calm the nerves."

"No thanks."

"Some gum, then?" He took out a pack. "Or how about . . ." He rummaged in the bag and lifted out a red box. "A strawberry and cream toffee? Made in England. Callard and Bowser, London."

"Come on, Ralph!"

"What . . . ?"

"Chewing gum, candy!" She laughed. "I hope you don't think I'm a little girl. I mean . . . I'm not."

"I'm quite aware of that."

"Good. I was afraid you were going to offer me a comic book next."

He unwrapped a toffee, ate it. "You're about—" He hesitated. "Twenty-five?"

"Yes. About."

"And very big indeed. As tall as I am."

"What else am I?"

"You're wearing a fur coat." He touched her shoulder. "Aren't you going to take it off? You'll roast."

"No, I'm fine. Tell me more."

"You smoke foreign cigarettes."

"Gitanes." She opened the gold case, offered him one. He accepted it with deft fingers. She lit it for him.

"You've been in a swimming pool recently," he said.

"How did you know that?"

"Your hair." He sniffed. "Chlorine. It's even stronger than the cognac you've been drinking."

She took a piece of gum, unwrapped it, chewed it.

"I hope you're not offended, Charlotte . . ."

"No, no."

"You are."

"Of course not."

"I'm impossible!" His hands moved clumsily, upsetting the flight bag, spilling candy and gum. "Imagine telling a woman her breath stinks!"

She gathered up the bags and packages, put them back into the bag. Lying on her lap were five one-hundred-dollar bills, held together with a paper clip.

"It's my beak," he said, pinching his hooked nose. "It leads me on. I can smell impending rain, earthquakes, hurricanes, forest fires, changes of temperature. . . . Once, when I was a little boy, down in Tijuana, I—it—saved my mother's life. We were picnicking out in the woods and I smelled a snake in the bushes. A grisly odor! Primeval! Awful!"

"How . . . ?" she began to ask, then hesitated.

"What?"

"Nothing."

"Please!" He put his hand on her arm.

"How long have you been like this?"

"Always."

The plane lurched wildly. Someone in a nearby seat yelped.

He squeezed her arm. "Don't be afraid," he whispered.

"I'm not afraid," she said, and put the money into his flight bag.

The Eye was sitting in an aft seat, finishing all the crosswords in his paperback. All except Number Seven. Fuck it. He put it away and opened a morning paper. The headline was impressive, but the facts were scanty. POLICEMAN

SHOT IN HOTEL SUITE. Irwin Sheen. Forty-six years old. Vernon Boulevard, Queens. Divorced wife. Two sons, eighteen and twenty-one. His own gun. Daphne Henry. Twenty-some years old. Iola, Kansas. Present whereabouts unknown. Sought for questioning.

There was no reference to the unknown guest in the room next to hers who disappeared at the same time she did, but he knew he was being "sought for questioning," too. The cops would never let a coincidence like that pass without an investigation. Fuck it. He'd registered at the Park Lane under an assumed name. He'd used another name when he bought his plane ticket. Daphne Henry never really existed. Neither did Erica Leigh. Neither did he.

He rang the stewardess and ordered a cognac.

Fuck it.

They came out of the airport building and stood in the warm sunshine. Forbes touched her.

"You're still wearing your mink? Take it off, for God's sake!"

"I can't." She smiled.

"Why not?"

A uniformed chauffeur walked up to them.

"Good morning, Mr. Forbes."

"Is that you, Jake?"

"Yes, sir. Sorry I'm late."

"That's quite all right. I'm in good hands. Jake, this is Miss Vincent. We're dropping her off at her hotel."

"Yes, sir."

The Eye watched them drive away in a Bentley.

She stayed for three weeks at the Beverly Wilshire. She bought a new wardrobe and a car. An MG. She had lunch with Ralph Forbes almost every day. They went out together every night.

He lived in a chateau on Benedict Canyon. His grandfather had come to California in the 1900s and had made a fortune in orange grove real estate. There was a street named after him in downtown LA. His son had married a girl with oil money. Ralph had a factory in San Bernardino—Forbes Sportswear, Inc. There was a Forbes Cosmet-

ics in Burbank, owned by his sister, Joan. There was a
Forbes Gallery on Sunset, operated by his brother Ted. Another brother, Basil, was a TV vice-president. Their uncle
was a DA.

Charlotte Vincent met them all. She was really coming
out in the open now, but very demurely. Nonetheless, the
Eye was worried. If she planned to follow her usual proce-
dure, she wouldn't get far this time.

In October she rented a small house on Oak Drive. She
furnished it sparsely, like an ascetic's temple, room by
room—a few chairs, two paintings, some rugs, a bed, a table with benches, a settee, a rocking chair. Ralph gave her
a three-hundred-dollar Dual 1249, and she began buying
records. Bach, Verdi, Ravel, Shakespeare, Chopin. Ted
Forbes was responsible for the paintings—a Thomas Eakins and a William Parker. Joan Forbes gave her a case of
champagne. One evening they all had dinner there together—Ralph, Joan, Ted, Basil, and Charlotte. Charlotte
cooked a *navarin aux navets nouveaux* and served a *tarte
au citron meringuée* for dessert. Afterwards they went to a
movie in Hollywood. Ralph and the chauffeur, Jake,
brought Charlotte home at midnight and left her at the
door. She sat up all night in the living room, smoking Gitanes.

There was nowhere in the neighborhood where the Eye
could hide, so he moved into a rooming house on La Cienega, two blocks away. He had a car now, too, but since he
couldn't drive up and down her street a dozen times a day
without attracting attention, he became a nanny.

He bought a wig. And a dress, a pair of pumps, a cape,
and a bonnet. And he trudged back and forth along Oak
Lane and Oak Drive every morning and afternoon, pushing
a baby carriage containing a make-believe infant past her
house.

At first he felt grotesque, like an ungainly transvestite.
But there were several other nursemaids meandering
through the streets with strollers, and he looked no more
outlandish than they did. He blended into their procession,
being careful never to approach any of them too closely.

Then faraway memories stirred. He began to imagine he
was a father again, that the empty bundle in the buggy was

little Maggie. She was four months old, wrapped in bright wool, unsmiling, staring at him with wide, solemn azure eyes. Long-forgotten images and aromas came back to him . . . his tiny, almost inexistent daughter in her crib, in her bath, in lamplight, in darkness . . . her baptism, her tantrums, her bottles and powders and ointments, her fevers, her sleep, her wakings. . . . It had passed so quickly, all that! He had hardly known her. There really hadn't been time enough for remembrances.

Then one day she was gone.

But now she had returned. He'd found her again, as he always knew he would—in Beverly Hills of all places! She grew older . . . six months, ten months, fifteen months . . . her wrinkled red newborn rawness vanished, she became smooth and shining, golden and solar. She began repeating the words he taught her: *tree . . . street . . . hand . . . daddy . . . sky. . . .*

He bought her a rattle and a rag doll in a shop on Wilshire.

He knew he was gone fucking nutty, but he didn't care. His happiness was too acute; it anesthetized everything else.

He made a pact with her, a covenant that was the crowning point of all this madness. He asked her to promise him she would haunt him when she died—as often as she liked, but at least just *once*, so he would know she was dead and could stop searching for her. She told him she would. They even picked a spot for the encounter—under an oak tree somewhere, at twilight, just before the lonely nighttime came.

And all the while he watched Charlotte. He saw her washing her car, opening and closing blinds, returning to the house carrying shopping bags, walking through her rooms, standing in the yard with her hands on her hips.

At night he discarded his disguise and crouched behind her garage, peering through her windows.

One night Forbes visited her and didn't go home.

They sat on the settee, watching TV together until eleven o'clock then she led him into her bedroom.

The Eye slept in his car and dreamed of the corridor lined with doors. In one of the classrooms a choir of children's voices sang a carol. He moved to a door and listened. He was afraid to open it, because he knew it would only lead him out of the school into other dreams. He rapped on it.

Maggie! he wailed. But maybe she didn't like to be called Maggie. Children often resented their names. *Margaret!* he shouted. No, this would never do! He was making too much noise. Someone would come and throw him out. He walked on, passing through an open gate. Now he was in a graveyard filled with goats. An old shepherd in a ragged confederate uniform sat on a tombstone, watching him.

You never did turn in that Minolta XK, he said. *Baker's going to be tear-assed if he loses one of his cameras.*

Is there a school around here anywhere? the Eye asked.

Yes, there is. Them children singing . . . can you hear them?

He woke at dawn and decided to break into the house.

In a used car lot in Glendale he found a battered old van. Painted on its sides were green triangles framing the white *W*s of *Wentworth Household Maintenance.* The dealer let him rent it for the day for fifty dollars.

At three o'clock he drove it along Oak Drive and turned boldly into her driveway. He parked before the garage, jumped out from behind the wheel carrying a tool kit. He was wearing khaki overalls and a cap. He walked to the back door of the house. It took him four minutes to spring the lock. He entered the kitchen.

He was sweating.

He stood for a moment by the sink until the pounding in his chest subsided. He turned on the tap, splashed water on his face. She was all around him, outraged, wrathful, screeching at him silently, her flailing arms beating him, fanning his ears like bat wings.

The kitchen was bare and spotless. A basket of pears sat on the counter of the breakfast gallery. Spread open beside it was a newspaper, the Capricorn section of the horoscope column encircled in crayon. He read it.

> . . . you Dec. 22–Jan. 20
> goat-people share birthdays
> with Katy Jurado (1924),
> Cary Grant (1904), Danny

Kaye (1913), Tippi Hedren
(1935), Guy Madison (1922),
Desi Arnaz Jr (1953), Dorothy
Provine (1937), Paul Scofield
(1922), Linda Blair (1959),
Ann Sothern (1911) . . .

He went into the living room and stood beside the rocking chair. He listened. She had either accepted his presence or had left to summon a flock of avenging Erinyes to drive him out. For the moment, though, there wasn't a sound.

He set the tool kit on the floor and glanced around. Five bottles of champagne stood on a shelf like a row of grenadiers. A book was lying on the settee—*The Mind of Proust* by F. C. Green. There was a *Paris-Match* on the table, an *Elle* on a bench. A pear sat by the telephone. A Parker on one wall, an Eakins on another. A pack of Gitanes on the windowsill.

He went into the bedroom.

Something tapped on the door as he opened it. He stopped, frozen. He advanced slowly. One of Ralph's canes was hanging on the knob.

The blinds were drawn. The air was heavy with scent. A zodiacal chart was tacked to the wall: Pisces, Aquarius, Capricorn, Sagittarius, Scorpio. . . .

A pipe sat in an ashtray on the bedside table. Did the sonofabitch smoke in bed? Did he lie there smoking his fucking pipe? A smoldering jealousy stabbed him. The prick! The blind cocksucker! Smoking his motherfucking pipe, stretched out between the clean cool sheets, his scrawny, blotchy carcass oozing and rumbling. . . .

He leaned against the wall, sputtering with anger. Hold it! Hold it! Fuck all! He wiped his face with his sleeve and went into the bathroom. Christalmighty! Wow!

He dropped to his knees and vomited in the toilet. Christ! Jesus! Oooooh! Man! He filled the bowl with thick, sickening offal. Ugh! He pulled himself up and flushed away the mess. Balls! He plugged the sink, turned on the tap, plunged his face in the water, opened his mouth. His knees almost gave way beneath him. God damn! He pulled out the plug. Shit! He washed his hands, wiped the smears from the metal. There were two toothbrushes in a glass on the shelf.

Holy Moses! This hadn't happened to him since—when was it? Oh, yeah—when his wife and Maggie left. Then again when he'd gotten that fucking photo in the mail. . . .

He went back past the bed and out into the living room, his legs jerking.

Well, anyway, if they were living together, she couldn't very well be wearing gloves in the house. Right? His mouth tasted like Sitting Bull's jockstrap! He ate a pear. Then he opened the tool kit, took out a bottle of powder, a brush, a spool of adhesive cellophane, several blank white cards.

He powdered the door of the refrigerator, the surface of the Dual, the arms of the rocking chair, the telephone, several glasses, a drawer, the frame of the Parker. There were latents everywhere, clean and neat. Were they his or hers though? Or someone else's?

Then he found it. Under the *Match* on a corner of the tabletop was a perfect left handprint—three fingers and the thumb, but no index. He taped the digits, transferred each to a separate card.

He dusted everything with a chamois rag, repacked the kit. He left, locking the kitchen door behind him. He climbed into the van and backed down the driveway to the street. It was three twenty-nine. He'd been inside the house exactly eighteen minutes.

The West Coast branch of Watchmen, Inc., was in a new high-rise on Central Avenue. The girl in charge of records was an ex-policewoman named Gomez. He was amazed that she remembered him. Not only that, but she seemed genuinely pleased to see him.

"Well, well! When did you get in, stranger?"

"Last night. How are you, Miss Gomez?"

"Up and down, like the stock market. Hey! We had an all-points telex on you last month, pal. Baker is looking for you like wild."

"He probably just wants to wish me a happy New Year."

"So do I."

"The same to you." He gave her the fingerprint cards.

"Can you drop these through the slot for me, Miss Gomez?"

"Sure thing."

"How long will it take?"

"A couple of hours."

He went back to his room at the Del Rio and sat staring out the window. Balls! He'd have to do something about Baker. He couldn't just stay out of the office forever without some goddamned explanation. He called him up.

"You shithead! Where the fuck are you?"

"In Los Angeles. At the airport."

"Listen—"

"Hello?"

"Hello! Listen, you schmuck—"

"Hello! I can't hear you!"

"Paul Hugo!!! What about Paul Hugo?"

"He changed his name. He calls himself Gregory Finch now. He spent a week in Montreal, two weeks in Ottawa, a week in Seattle and a month in Butte, Montana. He's in LA now, catching a plane for Rome. Me, too."

"Rome?"

"Hello?"

"What's going on? Rome? Look, god damn it to hell, I just can't stall his parents any longer! They want to turn the whole thing over to the FBI! Another thing! Do you still have that Minolta XK you checked out? Hello!"

"They're calling my flight! See you!"

He hung up.

He was back in Miss Gomez's office at six.

"She's got a record!" she announced happily. Records people were always delighted to unearth felonies. "New York State."

"Does she?" He was shaking like a leaf. He hid his hands behind his back. "Is she wanted for anything, Miss Gomez?"

"Nope. She pulled her time." She opened a folder, pulled out a Watchmen rap sheet. He took it, snatching it away from her quickly to cover his trembling.

He tried to read it. It was a blur.

"We're closing," she said. "Come on, I'll buy you a drink."

"I'd like that." He rubbed his eyes. "But some other time. I have to be in—in—I'm meeting somebody in five minutes."

He folded the sheet and hurried out to the elevators, feeling like Dolly Madison fleeing from the burning White House clutching the Declaration of Independence. Jesus! He had to take a leak! She had a record. No wonder she wore gloves. What would Baker do now? What could he do? Nothing! Of course she wore gloves. She pulled time. That meant there was a mug shot of her on file, and if they identified her they could circulate it. Hold it, though! There were pictures of Josephine Brunswick in existence, too. What about those photographers at the wedding when she married Dr. Brice? Those shots could be put into circulation. If they found Brice's body. Christ! It would take only one little push to bring the whole fucking house of cards tumbling down on her head. Capricorns must be fanatical gamblers.

Two women on the elevator edged away from him, incommoded by this fidgeting. Fuck them. And fuck Baker, too. Wow! He had to take a monumental leak! It was abominable!

Down in the lobby he found a john. Then he went outside and sat on a bench on Central Avenue. No, hold it, Gomez might find him here. He got into his car and drove all the way to the Hollywood Bowl.

He parked on a remote slope, still trembling. He sat there a moment, tapping his fingers on the windshield. Then he read the rap sheet, holding his thumb over the first line, covering her name.

NAME

DATE OF BIRTH   December 24, 1952

PLACE OF BIRTH   Trenton, N.J.

ADDRESS REFERENCES 1952–63, 127 Tyler Street, Trenton, N.J. 1963–70, Mercer County Home for Girls, Mercerville, N.J. 1970–71 Incarceration 1971–present X

PLACE OF CONVICTION   White Plains, N.Y. 1970

*CHARGE & SENTENCE   automobile robbery 13
months, Women's Detention Farm, Norwich, N.Y.
Aug 70–May 71*

Motors howled. A dozen boys and girls on bikes came
bouncing along the road. They wore goggles, football helmets, and leather jackets blazoned with red stars. They
passed in a typhoon of dust and noise.

The Eye lifted his thumb and read her real name.
JOANNA ERIS.

Seven

In December she had leased an empty shop downtown—a
small, modern, brick-and-glass oblong on Hope Street. Almost overnight it became a bookstore. The Librairie.

Just across the street was a hotel, the Del Rio. The Eye
moved into an upstairs front room, keeping his place at the
La Cienega rooming house as well.

During the shop's renovation, she would arrive in the
morning and stay there all day, supervising painters and
carpenters and electricians. At one o'clock the Bentley
would drive up, and she and Ralph would have lunch together. They'd come back at two and the work would continue, Ralph seated in a corner, trying to keep out of everybody's way. The chauffeur, Jake, would remove his tunic
and spend the afternoon sawing boards and hammering
nails. The only problem they had was with the gangs of
bikers roaring up and down the street, terrorizing pedestrians and occasionally throwing something through a window.

The Eye sat in his room, watching all this through binoculars.

On opening day, all the Forbeses were there, popping champagne corks and distributing trays of sandwiches. Charlotte and Joan placed portraits of Proust and Hemingway, Conan Doyle and Joyce in the display windows. Basil sat on a stool, playing folk songs on a zither. Ted stood outside, inviting passersby to come in for a drink. A bestselling author, a friend of Ralph's, breezed in and autographed copies of his latest novel. A crowd gathered on the sidewalk. Two movie stars showed up and had their pictures taken.

By noon over a thousand customers had bought books, emptying half the shelves.

It was Christmas Eve, Joanna Eris's birthday.

That night the Eye moved through the blackness of the yard to the living room window. Forbes was on the settee, drinking a cognac, smoking his pipe.

Joanna walked past him. She was holding his cane, twirling it.

"I wanted to be a majorette," she said. "But we couldn't afford it. The uniform cost fifty dollars. That was way beyond our means." She tossed the cane into the air, caught it. "I used to practice for hours. With a stick. Daddy kept promising me that just as soon as we had some money in the bank everything would be all right. But we never had any money in the bank and nothing was ever all right."

Ralph said something.

"He was everything," she continued. "A plumber, a truck driver, a paper hanger. Name it. Bartender, TV repairman, gardener, garbage man, bricklayer. Everything and nothing. One summer—" Her voice broke; she coughed. "One summer he sold encyclopedias from door to door. Or tried to. Never sold any." She whirled the cane, dropped it. "The worst job he ever had—oh, that was really awful! He was the chief usher at the Mayfair. God!" She picked up the cane, set it on a chair. "The Mayfair was a movie theater on Broad Street. He wore a red uniform with big buttons and epaulets and a cloak—a mauve cloak—and a little round hat. . . ."

She walked to the window. The Eye dropped to his knees. "He took tickets in the lobby, and looked absolutely ridiculous! Like a—a—I don't know what." She went over to the Dual, turned it on. She took a record from the rack. "It was bad enough when he was a plumber and used to come home smelling like shit. But that uniform! All my girl friends at school saw him, my teachers, the neighbors."

The record was playing. "But then, thank God, he was fired . . . as usual. That was the fall my mother died, in September. And there we were, just the two of us. He didn't work at all then. We were totally broke. September. October. November."

She wandered across the room, rubbing her hands, pinching her bent finger. "December. We were going to be evicted. One afternoon a man came and turned off our gas and electricity. It was my birthday. The twenty-fourth of December. I was eleven years old. Daddy bought a tree somehow, and we decorated it with strips of paper. An old woman who lived down the block—Mrs. Keegan—gave me some pears. That was our supper. Then we went out for a walk. We just roamed the streets like a couple of derelicts, looking at the lights. It was snowing, and people were still shopping. There were guys in Santa Claus outfits standing on the corners, ringing bells. I was frozen. We went into a department store to get warm."

She walked to the Dual and replayed the record. "This was playing on the loudspeaker. 'La Paloma.' " She stared at the turning record. "It was so incredibly lovely! The most beautiful song I ever heard. It made me cry. He thought I was crying because he . . . because he . . . I was standing there sobbing, you see, and he thought it was because he couldn't give me a present. So he said, 'Wait a minute, I'll get you something.' The poor man! He tried to steal a sweater and they caught him. I ran out of the store. I went home and waited for him. I waited all night. The next morning two detectives came and told me he was dead."

She walked past the window. "He was *dead*. He had a heart attack at the police station. He just . . . he. . . ." Her mouth opened. She bit her finger. A rasp of sorrow deep down in her throat shook her body. She dropped to the floor and sat on the rug, wild-eyed, streaming with tears.

Ralph got to his feet and came forward, groping for her. He collided with a chair, knocked it over.

"Charlotte!"

His searching hands found her, seized her. He sank beside her, took her in his arms.

She leaned against him, wailing softly.

"I can't wait until judgment day," she moaned, "when I can stand before God and tell Him how much I loathe Him!"

The Eye walked off to the street.

He spent the rest of Christmas Eve in a bar on La Cienega, drinking beer and doing a crossword puzzle. At two in the morning he drove around LA, watching the merrymakers. He parked his car on Fifth Street and sat on the front steps of the library for an hour. A hooker, then a fag, then another hooker tried to pick him up. He walked past The Librairie on Hope Street and looked at the books and portraits in the window. He had a cup of coffee in an all-night place on Grand Avenue. There were Christmas cards on display at the cashier's desk. He bought one of them. It was Norwegian. VELKOMMEN DEILIGE JULEFEST! He took out his pen and wrote on the inner flap:

> Long time no see. What are
> you up to? I miss you terribly.
> I hope you're happy. Please
> don't forget me. I want so much
> to see you, but I know I never will.
> Merry Christmas.
>
> Daddy

He addressed the envelope to Maggie, c/o American Express, Ulan Bator, Mongolia, and dropped it in a mailbox on Pershing Square.

The next day he flew to New Jersey.

The Mercer County Home for Girls was pure Charles Dickens. Grimy walls, a soot-smirched courtyard, dirty windows, dungeon archways. It looked like a Victorian flashback.

1963–70

Joanna Eris.

A column of little girls in gray smocks marched out of a shed, all carrying buckets. Several others were sweeping a hallway. Two more were changing the tire of a truck jacked up in the yard.

A thin, bald, erased-looking fellow wearing what looked like a streetcar conductor's uniform led the Eye through a passageway. He knocked respectfully on a door, ushered him into the lair of an old woman named Mrs. Hutch.

She was in her seventies, walrus-necked, puffy, mean, carnivorous.

"Joanna Eris? I remember her, yes." She didn't invite him to sit down. "What about her?"

"My company is trying to trace her. A deceased uncle in West Virginia left her some insurance money."

He gave her one of his bogus cards. She didn't bother to take it.

"She's probably in Sing Sing."

"Is that where your alumnae usually end up, Mrs. Hutch?"

"In the last five years, Mr. Wiseacre"—she picked up a ruler, moved it from the left to the right side of her desk— "fifteen hundred and thirty-six young ladies were discharged from this institution, and they are all now gainfully employed, every one of them."

"That's remarkable."

"I think so, too. We're very proud of our record. One of our alumnae, as you call them, is now in the State House, the private secretary of the governor of New Jersey. Another is a Bell Telephone supervisor, in charge of one hundred switchboards."

"And Joanna Eris?"

"Joanna Eris"—she picked up a pencil, moved it—"was one of our rare dropouts. She left here when she was eighteen. And a good riddance!"

"You didn't like her, Mrs. Hutch?"

"She was a troublemaker and a sneak. Insubordinate, vicious. A foul-mouthed, cat-eyed little misfit."

"Where did she go when she left?"

"To Trenton. She worked for two months with General Motors. Then she was fired. The personnel manager called me up one day and said, 'I'm sorry, Mrs. Hutch, I just cannot keep her on.' And he asked me if she was retarded."

"What did you tell him?"

"I told him the matter was no concern of mine." She moved the ruler back from the right to the left side of her desk. "Then she went to New York and was arrested for theft." Her counterfeit grandmother's head sank deeper into her blubbery neck, and she looked at him with hooded eyes. "Is this really about insurance?" she asked.

He was completely taken aback. "I don't understand, Mrs. Hutch. . . ."

"You wouldn't be"—she smiled bleakly—"fishing by any chance, would you?"

"Fishing?"

"Going to try to bring a lawsuit against the home after all these years?" He laughed flatly. "She told me she'd sue me one day. Wouldn't put it past her. Brazen little minx." He had no idea what she was talking about. He waited.

"It was her own fault. Just like that business with the electricity. Almost got herself electrocuted playing with the fuses. Blew the lights out all over Mercerville. Or when she was working in the kitchen. She left the gas turned on all night once. Could've killed us all."

She moved a paperweight on the desk. "She was always demolishing things. She was clumsy, inept, incapable of touching anything without smashing it. She ruined three sewing machines. Had to replace them. Put her elbow through the window of the greenhouse, had to have five stitches. If I were to send her a bill for all the damage she caused, it would cost her a fortune. She had nobody but herself to blame for her hand."

"Her hand? Do you mean her finger?"

"Just carelessness."

"How did it happen?"

"You see? You're fishing."

"No I'm not."

"If you are, say so"—she pointed to the telephone—"and I'll call our attorney."

"I'm not fishing, Mrs. Hutch. How did it happen?"

"A sickle."

"A sickle?"

"Cutting grass."

He looked past her. Hanging on the wall behind the desk was a dusty oil portrait of a pretty woman with a shy, frightened face. "Who's that?" he asked.

She turned, looked up. "Me." Her mouth twisted. "One of our girls painted it. In 1929. The year of the Crash. Herbert Hoover. Everybody was on relief, but my girls ate three square meals a day. They had coal in the winter and a week in Atlantic City every summer. Nobody remembers the Depression now. It didn't last long, thank the Lord. Everything passes." She moved a pair of scissors across the desk. "Time passes. I wonder what Joanna looks like today. The little bitch."

She broke wind gently, filling the room with the rank odor of locomotive smoke.

The Eye went back to Trenton.

He walked down Tyler Street.

Number 127 was a small, square, livid wooden house next door to a grocery store. The railing of the front porch was broken. The windows were open, a TV voice was laughing and chattering in the living room.

A young black came out the door. "Can I help you, stuff?"

The Eye hesitated. What was that name Joanna had mentioned? "I'm looking for—" What the hell was it? The old woman who gave her the pears. "Mrs. Higgins."

"Don't know her."

"No—hold it. Mrs. Keegan."

"Oh, her. Lived up the block. Dead and gone long ago. Passed off when I was just a pygmy."

"How long have you been here?"

"What's it to you, man?"

"Nothing. Just curious." More blacks were standing around now, watching him blankly. Four . . . five . . . eight . . . ten of them. On the sidewalk, in the street, on nearby porches. "I used to know the family who lived in one twenty-seven. Mr. Eris and his daughter. Did you know them?"

"When was that?"

"The fifties and early sixties."

"No way at all!" he giggled. "This was honk territory then. The Zulus have taken over since, as you can see."

A huge man in a turtleneck sweater strolled up to the Eye, playing to the crowd. "You want somethin', you?"

"No, I don't want anything."

"Then why don't ya just keep walkin'?"

He caught the noon train to New York. He drove to White Plains, first to the courthouse, where he read a transcript of her trial, then to a service station on Hudson Avenue, where he talked to a hunchbacked mechanic standing in a grease pit. His name was Zalesney.

"Yeah, Joey. Sure," he said wistfully. "Real good-looking chick. Wearin' them white overalls, the guys really honked their horns. She didn't last very long. Couple of months. She worked in the office, with Mr. Wozniak. And at the pumps when we was rushed. One day she climbed into a brand new Lancia Scorpion and just took off. The state cops busted her away up around Albany somewhere. The guy who owned the heap was tear-assed. He made the DA ram it to her, the prick. I don't know why they had to make such a big deal about it. She was just takin' a spin. She'd of probably brung it back. They gave her thirteen months."

The Eye drove to Norwich and had a look at the Women's Detention Farm. It was a village of immaculate white buildings in a hundred acres of woods and pastures. Girls in olive drab suits were driving tractors and marching around carrying shovels on their shoulders. From a distance they looked like soldiers.

A guard at the gate phoned the administration building and a few minutes later a warder in a Jeep drove out to talk to the Eye. His name was Giulianello.

"*Time* magazine." The Eye gave him one of his fake cards. "I'd like to interview your shrink."

"Shrink?" Giulianello blinked at him.

"You have one, don't you?"

"Yes, sir. Dr. Brockhurst."

"We're doing a story on prison psychology. I'm handling the girls' detention angle in New York State."

"We couldn't let you in without authorization from Albany, sir. Besides, Dr. Brockhurst isn't here. He's lecturing at Yale this month."

"Well, I'll get in touch with him later then. And I'll check with Albany first."

"That would be best, sir. I have a three-year subscription to *Time*."

"Good for you. How long has Brockhurst been with you?"

"Since 'seventy-three."

"Who was it before that? Maybe if I could talk to his predecessor, I could miss all the red tape bit."

"That would be Dr. Darras," Giulianello said. "Martine Darras. She's in private practice now. In Boston."

The Eye spent the night in New York and took a morning shuttle flight to Boston. He found Dr. Martine Darras's St. James Avenue address in the phone book.

Her office was a tenth floor suite with inch-thick tempered-glass walls facing the John Hancock Tower. The waiting room was bare and blue, with one long low couch against the window and a zodiacal chart on the wall.

A young woman in a faultless garnet-colored Chanel tailleur came out of the inner office. She was about thirty-two, dark, exquisite, mirror-eyed. Hanging around her neck on a thin chain was a silver disc engraved with a Virgo symbol. She was holding a pack of Gitanes.

"We're closed," she said pleasantly. "It's Saturday."

"Dr. Darras?"

"Yes."

"You were the prison psychologist at the Norwich Detention Farm a few years ago."

"Yes, I was."

He decided not to lie to her. He gave her one of his Watchmen, Inc., cards. "I'm investigating one of the former inmates. Could you give me just a few minutes?"

"Who are you investigating?"

"Joanna Eris."

"Come in," she said.

Eight

"She was brought there in August, 1970. I processed her the day she arrived. That's what they called it—*processing*." She laughed.

"A few simpleminded tests to determine whether or not an inmate was a total moron. Most of the girls were. The place was a Babel of ignorant, illiterate, demented female hoods. Armed robbery, larceny, extortion, burglary. There were even a few counterfeiters. They were all phonies, putting on a Goody Twoshoes penitent act so they could pull their time at the farm instead of going behind walls. Being locked up with them was nauseating. What Sartre calls *huis clos*. Joanna's coming there was like a benediction. I didn't really get to know her, though, until I had her taken off the work gang."

They were sitting at either end of a long couch in the glacial blue room, facing the window. Before them the Hancock Tower reared up in the morning haze like a cliff of yellow ice.

"Our teachers always warned us," Dr. Darras said, "about falling in love with our patients. But there I was, in that putrid zoo, with that rabble . . . and suddenly she was standing before me like Joan of Arc. What could I do? Eris, Joanna. Number 643291. She was so clean and faultless and salutary. I used to watch her marching around the yard . . . standing in line . . . sitting in the auditorium and in the dining hall . . . I couldn't keep my eyes off

72

her. I would get up at five thirty just to hear her say 'Here!' when her name was called at roll call. There was a grisly dyke there who bullied everybody. She was a Seneca Indian doing ten years for manslaughter. I had her transferred to the psychopath ward at Bellevue when she started putting her claws out for Joanna. Ethical, hmm?"

"And why did you have Joanna taken off the work gang?" the Eye asked.

"She was with one of labor units, out in the fields, digging a drainage ditch. Suddenly she stopped working and just stood staring at the woods. The guards tried to make her go back to the ditch. They couldn't. They shouted at her and began shoving her around. There was no reaction at all. She was in a trance. When they brought her to the dispensary, she seemed to be in a state of catatonia. She couldn't speak or move. I put her to bed and gave her a shot of thiopental. I asked her what was bothering her. She said she saw something in the woods."

"What?"

"She refused to tell me. That is, she refused to tell me then, during that first session. I found out much later what it was. It took me months to drag it out of her."

"What did she see, Dr. Darras?"

"A man was standing under the trees, watching her. It was her dead father obviously. They'd been very close. She refused to accept his death. Well, to make a long story short—" She got up and walked aimlessly across the room. "I put her through a—oh, a very superficial analysis. I found rage and hostility, hate and melancholia. What else would you like to know?"

"Virgo," he said.

"I beg your pardon?"

"Your zodiac sign." He pointed to the disc on her breast. "Yes."

"She's a Capricorn."

"I know. That was my doing, bringing that out. I got her interested in astrology to keep her mind occupied. And—"

"And what?"

"Music. There was quite a good record library at the farm. I made her listen to classics, operas, jazz, everything. Anything that would wake her up, stimulate her, inspire her. I made her recite poetry. I taught her how to dance. And books. I made her read. She devoured hundreds of novels. Proust, Balzac, Dostoevski, Stendhal, Tolstoi. Would you care for a drink?" She opened a cabinet, took out a bottle of Gaston de Lagrange and two glasses.

"Are you wearing a wig?"

"Yes, I am." She poured two drinks. She sat down beside him and pulled off the wig, revealing short-cropped platinum hair. "I had her appointed librarian. That took her off the work gang." The limpid silvery effect of her eyes, the disc, and her hair blended, infusing her in argent tincture. She sipped the cognac.

"Did you uncover any suicidal tendencies?" he asked.

She stared at him. "You must know her very well."

"No . . . I don't know her at all. But when she was in that girls' home in Jersey, she put her arm through a window and had to have five stitches. On another occasion, she left the gas on all night in the kitchen."

"She tried to kill herself several times. She was almost electrocuted with some wires or something. And she cut herself with a sickle." She shuddered. "A sickle!"

He asked her suddenly, thinking not of the sickle but of the ledge, "Is suicide a form of insanity, Doctor? And hallll—" he stammered, "hallucinations and all that?" *Like Grunder in the alley*, he wanted to add, *disguised as Mephistopheles*.

She refilled her glass. "Insanity is merely unhappiness," she said. "The mind is like any other organ, it becomes contaminated by pollution. And suicide is just another variety of thiopental shots."

Her lips tightened with anger. "That goddamned girls' home almost finished her! Are you against capital punishment? I'd like to see all bastards who torment children drawn and quartered or disemboweled. . . ." Then she laughed and lit a Gitane. "And yet my own son left home the other day. . . . He said I persecuted him. He called me a sadist." She shrugged.

"How far did it go?"

"Haw far?" She blinked at him.

"You and Joanna."

She got up and stood before the window, looking down

at St. James Avenue. "I'm telling you all this and I shouldn't. It's absurd. This is how far it went." She moved to the end of the room, threw the cigarette in an ashtray. "We'd meet in the library every night after the lights were turned off. I'd bring a bottle of cognac. We'd get undressed and get drunk. We'd dance. We'd sit on the floor and talk. Or play chess. I forgot to tell you, I also taught her to play chess, or tried to. It was a dismal failure. Then we'd make love. Only it was more like despair than love. Desolation. Another form of insanity and suicide."

"Have you seen her since she was released from prison?"

"No. Never." She walked back to the couch. "Tell me—what has she done?"

He rubbed his forehead tiredly, the exertion of the last few days finally catching up with him. "What did you tell her to do, Dr. Darras?"

"I?" She frowned. "I told her to confront life. To fight. Not to yield or grovel."

"Well, that's just what she's done."

On the flight back to LA he did the crossword puzzle in *The Boston Globe*. Then he read through some TWA folders. In one of them was an airlines chart of Europe. He studied a map of Czechoslovakia. There was only one city indicated, Prague (Praha), serviced by an Air France connecting flight from Paris. He pulled out his paperback and opened it to Puzzle Number Seven. *Capital in Czechoslovakia.* Four letters. But he was too weary to go through all that again. He'd thrown the book away twice, and twice he'd retrieved it to try once more to break the goddamned thing. He'd crack it sooner or later. But not today.

He tossed it on the seat beside him and borrowed a *Los Angeles Times* from a woman sitting across the aisle. He read about the economy. He read about the decline of steel production. He read about Soviet missiles, about the *Programme Commun* in France and racism in Rhodesia. He read the society page. *Miss Charlotte Vincent and Mr. Ralph Forbes announced their engagement yesterday at a party at the Mark Taper Forum. . . .*

He sat up, wide awake. *The wedding is scheduled for April. . . .* There was a photo of the couple, leaning

against a stairway ramp, smiling. Fuck! She might just as
well have been standing in a New York Police Headquarters lineup! Was she out of her mind? All any sharp-eyed
homicide cop had to do was glance at her and— No, wait.
He held the picture closer. She was wearing a shining Cardin evening gown, her head was wrapped in a turbanlike
bandeau. Her face was a lovely mask of bland anonymity.
She wasn't Daphne Henry. He had to admit that. No, she
was no one anybody in New York would recognize . . . or
anybody in Chicago, either, for that matter. *Miss Vincent
is from New Jersey.* . . . What gall! Dr. Darras would be
proud of her. *Mr. and Mrs. Paul Newman congratulated
the happy couple, as did Jodie Foster, Mr. and Mrs. War-
ner LeRoy, Lily Tomlin, LeVar Burton, Gore Vidal.* . . .
A gala of future witnesses!

*Would the defendant please stand. Mr. Newman, do you
recognize this woman?*

I do.

*Is she the same woman known to you as Mrs. Ralph
Forbes, alias Charlotte Vincent?*

She is.

*Objection! The prosecution is testifying for the witness.
Sustained.*

*Mr. Newman, would you tell the court in your own
words who this woman is?*

*She's Mrs. Forbes. The widow of Ralph Forbes. Like
you say, alias Charlotte Vincent.*

Jesus! She couldn't go through with it this time. It was
too insane.

He'd have to stop her.

An accident on the freeway blocked traffic for over an
hour. It was after eight when he got back to Hope Street.
The Librairie was closed. He made sure he still had his
room at the Del Rio, then drove to Beverly Hills.

Stop her? *How?* He had until April to find a way. Or
had he? Maybe she intended to make her move before the
marriage. An overnight drive somewhere . . . to the desert or the mountains or a beach. A blind man wasn't difficult to kill.

Maybe he was dead already. She could be gone by now.

That trip to Trenton had been sheer idiocy! She'd been alone for three whole days!

He drove along Oak Drive, slowing down as he passed the house. He sagged with relief. The Bentley was parked at the curb.

But it was only a reprieve. What about tomorrow? No, he couldn't wait until April. He had no idea when or where or how she planned to do it. Her whole pattern had been chaotic ever since she came to LA.

He turned into Oak Lane, drove up Ledoux, cut back to Oak Drive via Stanley Terrace.

Joanna Eris, Ralph, and the chauffeur came out of the house. The two men climbed into the Bentley and drove off. She went back inside.

He parked in the lane and walked through the familiar dark maze of pathways to the rear of the house. He slipped past the garage into the shrubs to the living room window.

She was sitting in the rocking chair, whistling softly.

He smiled and relaxed. He was home again.

She kicked off her shoes, lifted her skirt, rolled down her stockings.

They were together. Nothing else mattered for the moment.

She got up, unzipped her dress, peeled it off. She sat on the settee and removed her bra.

He loosened his tie, leaned comfortably against the wall. Together. Indivisible. All the rest was unimportant.

She yawned and stroked her breasts. His palms became heavy with the warmth of her flesh, her nipples greeting his fingers like old friends. He purred with pleasure.

She went to bed at midnight. He drove to La Cienega and spent the night in his rooming house.

He dreamed of the corridor again. All the doors opened for him, but it was Sunday and the classrooms were empty.

All but one.

In the same bare dank chamber where he once met the Leper King, he found old Mrs. Hutch writing on a blackboard.

Your daughter is no longer here, Mr. Wiseacre, she told him. *She is now gainfully employed as an embalmer in a funeral parlor*. And she laughed like a jackal. *One of these*

*days a corpse will be brought before her. It will be you.
She'll prepare you for burial, never knowing it's her daddy's body she's putting in the box. Time passes. Nothing
remains. Except old photographs of young faces.*

He looked past her. Printed on the blackboard was the
word *CZECHOSLOVAKIA*. And he suddenly saw the solution to Crossword Puzzle Number Seven. Holy Moses!
There it was! Right there in front of him!

Mrs. Hutch erased it quickly. *Never mind that*, she said.
You know what you have to do.

He woke with a start. He knew indeed! There was only
one way of stopping her from killing Ralph Forbes.

At nine o'clock she backed her MG out of the garage
and drove to Benedict Canyon. She spend all day Sunday
concealed behind the high walls of Ralph's Colosseum.

At seven thirty they drove to Santa Monica and had dinner at Nero's. She brought him home at ten.

The Eye walked through a black hollow behind the estate. He climbed over the wall, dropped down into an orchard. He moved through the trees, his radar fondling the
darkness for traps.

He felt a faint pulse of danger . . . a mere rustling in
the grass. He stopped, listened. A snake? A dog? There it
was again! He waited. A tiny hedgehog ran across a patch
of moonlight in front of him.

He moved on. He found a paved footpath, followed it
past a tennis court and a pool. The house sprawled before
him, as inky as a mausoleum.

The MG was parked by the terrace. Joanna and Ralph
were standing beside it, laughing.

He melted into the shadows, watched them.

"But you have an enormous family," Joanna was saying.
"Aunts and cousins and uncles who never see one another
except at weddings and funerals. They've all been phoning
me, insisting on a big thing."

"I want a quiet wedding," Ralph said. "In a little church
in a village somewhere. We can invite them all here afterwards for the family bit."

"But why not give them a production number, if that's
what they like?"

"Listen, Charlotte, the idea of having all my relatives

present, sitting there in their pews, watching me walk to the altar, waiting for me to trip over something, just doesn't appeal to me."

"All right." She laughed. "But in that case, why wait then? Let's go right now."

"Go where?"

"I don't know. To San Luis Obispo or someplace."

"Tonight?"

"Sure."

"We can't. I have a meeting with the auditors in the morning."

"Tomorrow, then."

"Okay!" He took her in his arms. "Tomorrow afternoon. It's a date."

She backed away from him, pointing across the driveway. "Look!"

"I never look, sweetheart. What is it?"

"A hedgehog!" She came around the car, moving past a row of chrysanthemums. "He's in the bushes here," she called. "Isn't that a sign of good luck, Ralph?"

"Hedgehogs? Yes, I believe so. If you see one during the full moon or something."

"Is there a full moon tonight?" She picked up a stick, poked it around the Eye's shoes.

"How do I know? No, I think it's the first quarter. Are you sure it wasn't a rat?"

"I saw it. Right here. Does that mean I'll only be seventy-five percent lucky?

She drove away a few minutes later.

Ralph lit his pipe and tapped his cane on the terrace flagstones, walking toward the rear of the house. He stopped, leaned against a pillar. "I know you're there," he said. "What do you want?"

The Eye jumped back as the cane slashed past his face. He circled Ralph quickly, kicked him in the knee, knocking him down into the driveway. He sprang after him, aiming at his legs. He chopped the edge of his hand at his thigh, missed and hit his waist. Ralph flounced along the ground away from him, neighing with agony, hacking at him wildly with the cane. The Eye hammered him again, on the arm, breaking it. Ralph screamed and floundered. The Eye danced around him, pounded him on the calf. The blow was painful, but harmless. He had to break one of his legs.

He tried to grasp an ankle. The flailing cane forced him back. He chopped him on the hip, then on the kidneys. A leg! He had to have a goddamned leg! He swung at the thigh again, missed again, hit the left tibia.

Lights were going on in the windows. He tried one last desperate blow. It slammed into Ralph's shoe, sending him spinning like a rolling log across the lawn.

Someone was shouting on the terrace. The Eye ran around the back of the house, crossed a patio, scampered up a flight of brick steps. He tried to reckon his position. The orchard was east of the house. The back of the house faced north. He was moving west—straight toward Benedict Canyon. No way! He veered to the left—south. He passed a shed, a sundial, a beach umbrella, chairs, a swing. Left again—east. Hands applauded behind him—clap! clap! clap! Three bullets whistled past him. Fuck all! A rifle or a carbine! Breath blew in his ear. A muttering bumblebee almost touched his nose. Ricochets! He raced up a slope. Trees. The orchard. The wall. He scrambled up it, flopped over its coping, dropped. The black hollow closed around him.

"Hey! What's that!"

A flashlight went on. He saw two prone bare figures on a blanket under a willow.

"Is it the pigs, George?"

"Somebody jumped over the wall!"

He galloped past them.

"There he is!"

The beam followed him as he came out of the dip, lighting his way. He flew across a clearing, turned right—south—in an arroyo, right again—west—toward the bottom of Benedict.

Five minutes later he was safe in the womb of his car parked on Sunset.

He spent the morning sitting in the window of his room at the Del Rio, watching The Librairie through his binoculars.

Joanna arrived at eight, the other girl at eight fifteen. They made coffee on a hot plate. Joanna read the mail.

They unpacked a carton of books, placed one of them in the front window—*Roots*, by Alex Haley. A waiter from a restaurant down the street brought them a bag of buns and three pears. The first customer came into the store—a woman with a dog. She began filling a shopping basket with paperbacks—four . . . six . . . eight . . . ten . . . a dozen of them. The paperbacks were to the left, the hardcovers to the right, novels in the back, nonfiction in front. Along the rear wall was the counter. The deluxe editions were on several stands in the center of the store, and Joanna's desk was in an alcove just behind the novels.

More customers entered. They bought five copies of *Roots*. One of them bought a large Picasso volume in a gaudy jacket for fifteen dollars. The woman with the dog carried her basket of paperbacks to the cash register. She huddled over the counter, scratched a pen point on her tongue, wrote out a check. She tore it up, wrote out another. A girl in a cowboy hat bought a bulky dictionary—twenty-five dollars. A small boy bought a Tarzan album, paid for it with a handful of pennies and dimes. Now the woman's pen was out of ink. She shook it, dropped it, picked it up, licked it, scratched it on the counter. Joanna loaned her a ball point.

There was no mention of Ralph in the morning papers or on the nine o'clock news. The Eye hoped he was in the hospital, at least for a few weeks. A broken leg would have put him out of circulation much longer, but assaulting a blind man hadn't been as easy as he thought it would be. His arms and wrists were purple with cane marks.

Anyway, there would be no marriage this afternoon.

The binoculars pulled the bookstore closer, and Joanna was standing in front of him. She was leaning against the counter, one hand on her hip, the other holding the goat disc, spinning it between her fingers as she talked to a customer.

She turned suddenly and looked straight at the Eye.

She saw only the passing traffic and the hotel across the street.

"Is anything wrong?" the customer asked.

She laughed. "Somebody's walking over my grave."

The Bentley pulled up to the curb outside. Jake alighted

from it quickly and opened the rear door. Ralph climbed
out to the pavement. His arm was in a sling and one foot
was bundled in a heavy bandage. He was carrying a crutch.

The Eye rose from his chair, stunned, and ran downstairs to the lobby.

He came out on the sidewalk just as Joanna rushed out
of the store. She stood before Ralph, petrified with surprise. He tucked his crutch under his arm, laughing. He
kissed her, kicked his bandaged foot gaily. Jake was laughing too, gesturing, shadowboxing, jabbering.

The Eye crossed the street numbly.

Motors droned. A swarm of bikes flashed past him. He
whirled, saw the football helmets, the black jackets with
red stars, the hairy jowls, the bug-eyed goggles. A boy
rolled in front of him, inches away, his yaklike face glaring, his mouth slit open in a savage snarl.

The Eye ran.

The boy U-turned smartly, zoomed after him. The Eye
jumped across the pavement into a doorway. The bike
bounced behind him, howling like a fury. It hit Ralph,
sending him pirouetting with slapstick whimsicality along
the curb, then lifting him in the air and pitching him acro-
batically into the fenders of a passing car. The car dragged
him up the block, its brakes squealing.

Joanna ran to the crushed heap piled in the gutter. She
dropped atop it, screaming, pulling it into her arms.

And in that one terrible instant the Eye knew that she'd
never had any intention of killing Ralph Forbes.

On God's plotting board a tiny red light flashed on Hope
Street.

Nine

At the cemetery he stood in the back of the crowd behind a senator and a cluster of local politicians. Joanna remained in the background, too, on the rim of the family, unobtrusive and isolated, somberly dressed but not in flaunting mourning.

After the ceremony she drove home alone.

The Eye put on his nanny clothes and pushed the baby carriage past the house. She sat in the MG in the driveway, gazing at the garage doors. She climbed out listlessly and walked up the street toward Wilshire.

He followed her, the wheels of the carriage squeaking like crickets.

She crossed La Cienega, passed his rooming house. She bought a newspaper and stood on the corner of Gale reading her horoscope. He knew what the Capricorn column advised; he'd already read it.

> This is the winter of
> your discontent and all
> the planets lower upon you.
> A radical change of scene is
> recommended. Hail and farewell!

She walked all the way to the museum, then turned around and walked back. Then turned again, crossed Wilshire, and wandered up Hamilton to San Vicente. Then she came down La Cienega to Wilshire again and turned into

83

Ledoux. She came through Oak Lane to the Drive and
stopped. She stood with her hands on her hips, staring at
the house. She climbed into the MG and backed out of the
driveway.

The Eye ran to the Lane, breaking all baby-carriage
speed records. His car was parked on the corner of Ledoux. Two real nursemaids watched in amazement as he
folded the carriage and lifted it into the trunk. He sprang
behind the wheel and started the motor. It was four
o'clock. He was almost certain that she would go either to
the bookstore or to her bank. He drove to Olympic Boulevard.

The MG was just ahead of him, speeding toward Santa
Monica.

She went to the bank and emptied her safe-deposit box.
Then she drove to the bookstore. It was closed for the day.
She unlocked the front door and walked past the deluxe
displays to her desk behind the novels. She sat down, lit a
Gitane. The cash box was on the floor behind a potted
plant. She picked it up, set it on her lap, dialed its combi-
nation, opened it.

The Eye pulled off his nanny cap, his dress, the bonnet,
and his Mother Hubbard wig. He went into the Del Rio,
packed his bag, paid his bill, and checked out.

Across the street, Joanna left The Librairie without bothering to lock the door behind her.

She drove home.

He wondered if he had time to get his things out of the
La Cienega rooming house. But there was nothing of any
value there, except a favorite pair of shoes. He decided to
abandon them.

She carried two valises out of the house, put them into
the MG. She climbed behind the wheel and drove away.
She didn't look back.

Hail and farewell!

She spent two months driving around and around south-
ern California, staying at motels and resorts. San Diego, El
Centro, Lakeside, San Bernardino, San Ysidro, Escondido,
Oceanside, Elsinore, Redlands, back to San Bernardino,
back to El Centro. Up and down, in and out.

She had her hair cut. Her skin was burned copper from sunbathing. She wore slacks and sweaters and old jackets. She drank three, sometimes four, cognacs a day. She read her horoscope every morning. She read and reread *Hamlet* and marked its pages with green and red and orange and yellow felt pens. One afternoon, in a bar in La Jolla, she played "La Paloma" over and over again on the jukebox, seventeen times.

Then in March she drove back to LA, parked the MG, and flew to Las Vegas. She spent a month there as Miss Leonor Shelley.

She lost six thousand dollars shooting crap.

The syndicate soldier ants waved their antennae at her, but sensed some interdiction that made them leave her alone. Perhaps it was just an antique Italian foreboding of evil, a Tyrrhenian seashell echo-warning of *cattiveria*. They watched her, surrounding her with a deep moat of misgiving, but they never tried to move in. The Eye prayed that she wouldn't pull anything here. If she did, they would drive a stake through her heart and stuff her mouth with garlic. But as long as she behaved, her anonymity was impregnable and absolute.

He knew that they were watching him, too, and that they were perfectly aware of his and Miss Shelley's strange affiliation. They didn't try to explain it. They simply stood back and waited for both of them to move on.

The Eye enjoyed the experience. It was restful and safe. He didn't have to follow her twenty-four hours a day now. A bartender or pitman would always know exactly where she was and tell him if he asked.

He relaxed and took a vacation. He ate regularly and put on some weight. He slept soundly and dreamlessly. He worked out in a gym, played handball, swam, and won eighteen hundred dollars at roulette. He began enjoying Gitanes. He bought a copy of *Hamlet* and memorized it. His favorite passage was

> Leave her to heaven
> And to those thorns that in her bosom lodge
> To prick and sting her.

He enjoyed the long nights best of all, though—the taste of the desert on his pillow and the deep slumber without corridors and nightmares. He dreamed of Maggie only in the daytime, taking her with him to the pool, lunching with her, having breakfast with her on the terrace, meeting her on stifling afternoons in the street, and escaping with her into a cool movie or an ice cream place. Then she would disappear, and his longing would rack him mercilessly until she came back. And she always came back—always—walking across an intersection, waving to him, appearing suddenly out of the crowd and taking him by the hand, calling his name softly in the sunlight.

They spent more than thirty days together, almost constantly. He bought her a "Nevada" patch to sew on her sweater. He gave her coins to play the slots. When he realized that she was no longer a little girl but a young woman now, in her twenties—a woman indeed!—he tried to think of some fabulous gift he could offer her. A bracelet or a Lancia or a Saint Laurent dress or . . . but what the fuck did fathers give to daughters anyway, in homage and veneration? Finally, in the hotel jewelry shop, he had her zodiac sign engraved on a platinum disc and wore it around his neck for the rest of his life.

In April, when Joanna-Leonor's dice table losses amounted to sixty-two hundred dollars, she flew back to LA.

There was a riot at the airport when the plane landed. A task force of men and women wearing gas masks invaded the tarmac, waving signs reading *ABOLISH JETS! DANGER DON'T BREATHE! IT'S A GAS! SAVE OUR ENVIRONMENT!* The cops counterattacked. The Eye lost his hat in the brawl. A half-dozen people were thrown off a ramp and taken to the hospital in a fleet of ambulances. Joanna-Leonor was mashed against a wall; her dress was torn and there was blood on her arm. An airport doctor bandaged her.

She reclaimed the MG and drove north along the coast. She spent the night in Santa Maria and the following day swung inland. She drove through Paso Robles, Coalinga, Harford, and Selma. On the outskirts of Fresno she stopped at a wayside hopsital clinic and had her bandage changed.

The Eye drove past the clinic, turned into a side road,

stopped beside the fence of a golf course. He opened a *Chicago Sun-Times* he'd found on the plane and did the crossword puzzle.

That was the day the mockingbird sang—thank God! Otherwise he might have forgotten the entire incident. It began jeering at him from a nearby tree, ranting, like an insane flutist. A golfer walked up to the fence.

"You can't park here," he said pleasantly. "This is private property."

The Eye apologized. "I've been driving all day. I wanted to take a half-hour break."

"Well, go ahead, I guess. As long as you don't block the road." He walked off.

The Eye tried to concentrate on the puzzle, but the bird scoffed at him vehemently, bombarding him with rancor and scorn. He folded the paper and set it aside.

Joanna slept at a hotel in Fresno, registering as Diane Morrell. The next day she turned back toward the coast.

A few miles from Gilroy she parked on the shoulder of the highway and opened the MG's hood. The radiator was steaming; she tried to unfasten the cap and scorched her fingers. A dazzling new Porsche 927 pulled up behind her. A man in a pink cardigan jumped out.

"Don't bother with it," he said. "Throw it away and I'll buy you a new one."

The Eye slowed down, stopped beside them. "There's a garage up ahead," he called stupidly.

He couldn't for the life of him understand what made him do it. It was pure compulsion. They ignored him. They were bending into the MG's steam, laughing and quipping. He drove on.

Pink Cardigan roped the two cars together and pulled her into Gilroy. They left the MG at a garage and had a drink together in a roadhouse.

The Eye drifted in after them. He sat at the bar. They were at a corner table, wrapped in shadows. His radar was erratic again. Bad vibes!

He was calling her Diane. She called him Ken.

The room was almost deserted. Two husky tennis players in white shorts were standing at the bar, filling the place with a locker room stink. The bartender was arguing with somebody. The shutters were closed, covering the tables with a pall of murk.

Ken. Ken. Ken. The Eye knew him; he was certain of that, the vibes told him so. Kenneth. Kenley. Kendall. Indianapolis. St. Louis. Kansas City. A heavy. A hardcore case. A Southerner. He opened the filing cabinets of his mind and dug out armfuls of old records covered with cobwebs. Tennessee. North Carolina. Mississippi. Nashville. Memphis. Chattanooga. Rough stuff. Brutal. Nasty. A rebel.

He was doing most of the talking. Joanna-Diane just sat back and let him smother her in thick sorghum molasses guile. Ken. Ken.

"Did anybody ever tell you"—he put two cigarettes between his lips—"that you have eyes like a puma?"

"Pumatang," she laughed. "Pumatang eyes."

This stopped him cold for an instant. Then he smiled. "My goodness," he drawled. "How you do talk." He lit both cigarettes, gave her one.

"You're superb," she said. The Eye recognized the voice—the accent—the intonation—everything—even the irony. It was Dr. Martine Darras speaking. "Superb and formidable. And pink." She touched his cardigan sleeve. "Why do men insist on wearing pink?"

"My little sister knitted this for me." He took her wrist and looked at the bandage. "You cut yourself, honey girl?"

"I fell down," she said. "Skiing. In Chamonix. My daddy and I. I dropped into the deep snow covering the rocks. He pulled me out and wrapped his scarf around my arm. 'Can you hang on me?' he said. And he lifted me on his back and skied down the mountain. The awful people there . . . the snobs and the playboys . . . the ski bums and the millionaires and the sharpies . . . all the sneering smug people with faces like Babylonian idols . . . they were ashamed. Because they were incapable of doing such a thing themselves, you see. They would have left their daughters in the snow to smother and freeze."

He grinned, his even white teeth phosphorescent in the dimness. "Tell me more," he said.

The Eye went outside. The Porsche 927 was in a corner on the blind side of the parking area. He picked the lock of the trunk, lifted it open. A blanket covered the floor. He pulled it aside, revealing a Bowie knife in a rubber sheath, an army bayonet in a scabbard, a five-inch hunting knife, its point sticking in a cork, a moon knife, three king-sized switchblades, and a pair of brass knuckles. They were laid out in a neat row, like an array of butcher's tools in Dr. Frankenstein's laboratory.

Ken. Yes, he remembered him now. There was a shoe box, too; he opened it. It was filled with dozens of sachets, needles, a spoon, two syringes, and a jar of blue devils. He closed it, re-covered everything with the blanket.

His name was Dan Kenny. The Eye shut the trunk, re-locked it. Louisville, Kentucky. Dan "Ken Tuck" Kenny. Alias Kenny Tucker. A psycho. Three convictions—one stickup, one assault and battery, one homosexual bust. He'd been on the front pages for a week or so in 'seventy-six because of a lurid sexual aggression charge pressed by a male victim in Elkton. The case had never gotten to court.

At six thirty they went back to the garage. Then they drove off together, Kenny leading the way in the 927, Joanna following in the MG. They drove toward Santa Cruz and checked into a motel on Monterey Bay. It was going to be a wild night.

The Eye unpacked his .45, loaded it, stuck it in his belt. Their unit was the last in the block, in the dunes, separated from the beach by a high wire fence. He looked through the bathroom window. Joanna was sitting in the tub, leaning back tiredly, her face in her hands. A transistor sat on a chair beside her, playing Beethoven's C-Minor Piano Concerto. Her goat disc was lying on the sill, three inches from his forehead. He moved to another window.

"Diane!"

"Ho?"

"Hurry up, honey girl!"

"Hold your horses, motherfucker. Honey girl is in the middle of her ablutions."

In the bedroom "Ken Tuck" Kenny was pulling off his pink cardigan, chuckling. "How you talk!" He unbuttoned his shirt. Around his waist he was wearing a heavy money belt. He unbuckled it, dropped it on the floor behind the couch, walked to the shoe box sitting on the bureau, lifted off its lid, took out a syringe. He turned. Joanna's purse was on the bed. He went over to it, opened it, peeked into it. It was packed with money. He whistled. "What a doll!"

The Eye went back to the bathroom window. Joanna rose out of the tub, dripping all over the floor. "What?"

"I said, What a doll."

"I can't hear you."

"Doesn't matter none."

She pulled on a kimono, too weary to dry herself, picked up the disc, clasped it about her throat. She went into the bedroom.

The Eye glided to the other window. Kenny was no longer there. She walked over to the bureau and stood frowning at the syringe. She reached into the box, took out a needle. Where was Kenny? She went to the bed, opened her purse. The money was still there. She hissed with relief, rummaged, pulled out a tiny revolver. The Eye gaped. Where the hell did she get that? She must have picked it up in Vegas. She slipped it under the pillow. Where the fuck was Kenny?

He pivoted.

Kenny swung at him. He ducked. The fist swooped over the top of his head and thumped the wall. He ran. Kenny lurched after him, swinging at him again, bellowing. The brass knuckles grazed the Eye's shoulder, ripping open his jacket and lacerating his spine. He jumped up to the top of the fence, flopped over it, dropped, rolled down an incline of dunes. He somersaulted to his feet, raced along the beach.

Kenny laughed. "Asshole!" he shouted. He went back into the unit, quivering, elated, rocking on his heels. Joanna stared at the knuckles. He tossed them on the bed. "Just some little peeper outside," he wheezed. "Gettin' hisself an eyeful of the action." He fingered the front of her kimono. "Can't blame him. You look real cool and nice, honey darlin'."

She pointed to the syringe. "What's this, Ken?"

"It's for you, baby doll."

"Oh, no."

"Sure."

"Not me."

"I don't like to turn on alone."

"You go right ahead. I'll just watch."

"Just watch, eh?" He pushed her against the wall, grasping handfuls of her. "Watch the freaks. See them perform. A free floor show." He was bulging. He rubbed it against her. "It'll be something to tell your friends afterwards."

She tried to move past him. "I don't have any friends."

"Something to tell your daddy." He rammed his knee between her legs. "Ol' daddy."

"My daddy is dead."

She pushed him back, ran toward the bed for the gun. He hit her across the side of the head. She fell to the floor. He stepped on her hand.

"You like that? You want some more?" He struck her again, flattening her against the rug. "Huh? An' if you start yellin', I'll kick your teeth down your throat!" He leaned over and bit her on the rump. "Little ol' puma girl!" He jerked back the kimono, wiped his face on her thighs.

He left her lying there and went to the bureau. He pulled off his trousers, stroked his erection, slapped it playfully. He crumpled a piece of newspaper, dropped it in an ashtray, struck a match, set it on fire. He took a spoon from the shoe box, heated it on the flame.

He stuck a needle on the syringe, filled it. He danced over to her, bent down, rolled her on her back. He stabbed her arm, pushed in the piston.

Then he cooked another jolt for himself, injected it, and sat on the floor patting his penis until the charge hit him. He crawled over to Joanna, pulled off her kimono. He played with her toes, her nipples, her navel. He tried to enter her ear but lost his hardness. He put it in her hand and wiggled his hips until he was oblique again.

She gazed at him, scowling at the hair on his chest. He sat on her face, bounced up and down, tried to empty his bowels. Then he dropped forward on his elbows and listened.

Outside, a car motor was sputtering.

He pulled himself up, bounded to the door, unbolted it, jerked it open, rolled outside. The 927 and the MG were parked side by side in the yard. He ambled around them, trying to open their doors. They were both locked.

"You all there, now, hey!" he shouted. He stumbled back into the room, slammed the door, bolted it.

Joanna was crawling toward the bed. Squeaking with glee, he took her by the ankles and tugged her back across the floor. He went into the bathroom, sat down on the edge of the tub, took one of her stockings, squirmed lasciviously, pulled it on, holding his hairy leg in the air. Then he clipped her bra around his chest. He got up, shimmied out into the other room. He clapped his hands, jogged, warbled.

He cakewalked around the bed, hopped over Joanna—stopped. The Eye was leaning against the bureau, smiling at him. His arm flew out like a catapult, whipping the barrel of the .45 across Kenny's jaw, shattering his even white teeth and knocking him cold.

He threw back the bed covers, lifted Joanna gently, eased her naked body between the sheets. Her mouth spumed and she murmured, "Don't hurt her . . . please don't hurt her." She glared at him through the slits of her eyes, trying to rise, but he held her down until she passed out, then wet a washcloth and wiped her face.

He took the car keys from Kenny's trousers, unbolted and opened the door, dragged Kenny outside, unlocked the 927, dumped him into it.

He came back into the room, took the money belt from behind the couch. Its pouches were filled with tightly packed wads of one-hundred-dollar bills. He helped himself to twenty of them, left the rest on the pillow beside Joanna.

He gathered up the pink cardigan, the shirt and trousers, loafers and socks, Kenny's overnight bag and the shoe box, carried them outside, kicking the door shut behind him. He emptied the sachets on Kenny, scattered the needles and syringes around him, dropped the bag and clothing on top of him.

He climbed behind the wheel, released the brake, and rolled silently out to the highway. About five miles up the beach he parked in the dunes, unlocked the gas cap, and poured several handfuls of sand into the tank, then let the air out of two tires.

The sun was rising by the time he came into the yard of the motel.

The MG was no longer there.

He ran into the unit. The bed was empty. The money belt was gone. So was Joanna's luggage. So was Joanna.

Gone.

He stood there for a moment, looking around inanely. The brass knuckles were lying on the floor. He picked them up, reached under the pillow. The revolver was still there, too. He pocketed it and left.

An old woman in pajamas was standing on the porch, lighting a cheroot.

"Good morning," she said.

"The girl in number one eleven . . ."

"She just left."

"How long ago?"

"Twenty minutes."

"Which way did she go?"

"How the fuck do I know?" She waved toward the highway. "That way."

He got into his car and drove to the gate. He sat staring up and down the empty road. To the left was Santa Cruz, to the right Watsonville. Which way indeed! She could be halfway to San Francisco by now, or on her way back to LA.

He turned left. In Santa Cruz he bought a newspaper and checked the horoscope column.

> CAPRICORN. "Absence makes
> the heart grow fonder."
> You will lose nothing by
> going off by yourself for
> a while to think things over.
> Unknown shores beckon. Heed
> the call.

Ten

He drove to Los Gratos and San Jose. To Palo Alto, to Redwood City, to San Mateo. He drove everywhere, showing blow-ups of the Minolta photos to desk clerks, chambermaids, bartenders, waitresses, gas station mechanics, bus drivers, taxi drivers, hairdressers, railroad porters, newsboys.

Back in Beverly Hills the house on Oak Drive was still empty, a For Rent sign on the lawn. He telephoned Ted Forbes, pretending to be one of Charlotte Vincent's old school chums from New Jersey and asking him if he had her address.

"No, I haven't," Ted answered. "Charlotte left Los Angeles months ago. In March. We haven't seen her since."

"How can I get in touch with her?"

"I haven't the faintest idea. Sorry."

The Eye hadn't the faintest idea, either. He drove past the bookstore on Hope Street. It was now a barbershop.

He spent two months in Alameda, turning in endless circles, roaming the countryside, visiting Livermore, Tracy, Stockton, Sonora, Angel's Camp, Lodi, Rittsburg, Richmond, Berkeley, Oakland. He spent another month in San Francisco, checking thousands of hotels.

But he really had no reason to believe she was still in California. He just couldn't think of anywhere else to look for her, couldn't think of anything else to do. He'd get out of bed at six in the morning, thinking it was twilight, and drowse around in a daze until noon, waiting for the sun to set, then go back to bed and wake again at four or five, thinking it was dawn. One afternoon he found himself on Half Moon Beach and had no idea how he got there, one evening he fell asleep in his car in a parking lot in San Lorenzo, only to wake up five hours later on the other side of the bay in a bus terminal waiting room in Belmont. He looked in the mirror one morning and was astonished to see that he had a mustache.

He would lie on the floor for hours in his hotel room, surrounded by her photos, trying to evoke some living shape of the real Joanna from the myriad of artificial faces and wigs, trying to abstract some substance from her, something he could absorb for its nourishment of hope. His radar probes ranged in every direction, through hundreds of villages and cities, but she resisted him resolutely.

For three months, he didn't do a single crossword puzzle.

In August he read in the papers that three convicts had been killed in a cell block riot in a prison in San Jose. One of them was Dan "Ken Tuck" Kenny. He'd been serving a ten-year sentence on a narcotics rap.

In early September he finally faced the fact that he had failed. He either had to give it up or flip. So he shaved off his mustache and called Baker.

"No shit! I don't believe it!"

"I lost Paul Hugo, Mr. Baker."

"I've got two guys in Rome looking for both of you!"

"I'm not in Rome, I'm in Frisco."

"Frisco?!?"

"He flew to Cairo in May, then went to Hong Kong via Bombay and Singapore."

"You gotta be kidding me!"

"He came back to the States yesterday and I lost him this morning. What do I do now?"

"Call it off. His parents bought it last week in a car smash-up in Florida. No more client."

"That's too bad."

"Don't worry. Their last payment'll cover your expenses. How much have you been spending?"

"Something like . . . uhh . . . forty grand."

"Jesus H. Christ!"

"I tried to keep it down to a minimum, but—"

"All right. No sweat. Come on back."

"I'd like to take a couple of weeks off first. How about some bread?"

"See the local people. Let them handle the fucking book-keeping!" He hung up.

The Eye faked some vouchers on the hotel typewriter and took them to the Watchmen, Inc., office on Post Street. The cashier cleared everything by Telex and gave him a check for forty-five thousand dollars, which covered all his expenses for the last eight months three times over.

He deposited in a bank, bought two suits, a half-dozen shirts, a sweater, some ties, a pair of Hugo shoes (*Founded in 1867*), and a Harris Tweed topcoat. He traded in his car for a new VW Rabbit. He changed hotels. He drank three double cognacs. Then he went to bed and waited to see what would happen.

He was surprised to find himself suddenly back in the school corridor, trying to open the classroom doors. They were all locked, naturally. He was still playing in the same old B picture! He laughed with delight. He loved this movie! He'd seen it hundreds of times! The hero was a poor fink looking for his daughter, and he kept pounding on doors . . . it was hilarious! There was this classroom somewhere in the building and fifteen little girls were sitting at tables. One of them was Maggie . . . but he didn't know which one. She was hiding from him. Why? That was the mystery. *The Mystery of the Fifteen Tiny Pupils.* Anyway, the big scene—the denouement (ten letters meaning "the resolution of a doubtful series of occurrences")—was when he came barging into the room yelling, *Maggie! Hey, Maggie! Where are you?* and . . . Well, it was only a movie. He'd catch her between classes. During—what did they call it? Recess.

He sat down on a bench in the corridor and smoked a Gitane, waiting for the bell to ring. Facing him, hanging on the wall, were two towel racks, one marked His, the other Hers. He took out the paperback to finish Crossword Number Seven.

Czechoslovakia. Hold it! He knew the solution, but his pen was empty. He tried to scratch in the four letters, but it was impossible. No ink. But it didn't matter. He knew the goddamned solution, he'd just have to remember it when he woke up. It was the name of a saint beginning with a *J. St. John . . . St. James . . . St. Joseph . . . St. Joan . . . J . . . J . . .* Why *J*? Hospitaler! The Knights of St. John of Jerusalem! But what the fuck did that have to do with Czechoslovakia? Then her voice whispered in his ear, *Don't hurt her.*

He sat up, wide awake.

Rain was splashing on the windows. The lamp beside the bed was on. He switched it off. The damp grayness of dawn moistened the edges of the room.

Don't hurt her. She'd said that in the motel, just after he'd belted Kenny.

He got dressed and went down into the lobby. It was about six. The night clerk smiled at him miserably. "Good morning, sir."

"Good morning." He went outside and walked through the deserted leaden rainy streets. *Don't hurt her.* She was telling him where she was; it was all there in his B-picture dream, he was sure of that.

He sat down on a wet bench near the park.

She'd thought he was Kenny and she was pleading with him not to harm her. Her. Me. The objective case of *she* or the objective case of *I*? No! Shit! She'd said *her*—please don't hurt *her*! So she'd been talking about someone else. *Who?*

It would come.

He put it aside and tried to analyze the rest of the dream. The empty pen—that was obviously a Freudian bit. Sure. The inevitable cock. No ink. Impotency or sterility or something. The *J* was—what? A saint? *San* or *Santa*? One of the towns he'd searched recently? San Jose? San Juan? Santa Juanita? And the school and classrooms . . . the corridor and all that . . . that had been Maggie. Just a montage.

Hold it! Maybe not, though. There was a fucking subtlety in dreaming that wakefulness always ridiculed. Maggie. His daughter. The school. A building. A building filled with hidden children. Sonofabitch! It was coming! *J*! His and Hers Hospitaler! Don't hurt her!

"What're you doing, buddy?"

He turned. A tall cop was standing beside the bench.

"Toothache. Couldn't sleep." He held his jaw. "It's killing me."

"You live around here?"

"Hotel there."

The cop eyed the tweed coat and good shoes. "You need an aspirin. Vitamin B-1."

"Tried that. No way."

"What're you going to do?"

"See a dentist. Got an appointment for nine o'clock. Until then I just sweat it out."

"Well, don't get picked up for vagrancy." He walked off, chuckling.

The Eye jumped up and went into the park. God damn it! He'd lost it! It was all just a shambles now! Balls! He typed out a Watchmen, Inc., report card in his mind:

> Subject—Joanna Eris
>
> Comment—During the last X months, sometime in the course of my surveillance, subject visited a location situated in the town of San J. After her disappearance she in all probability returned to this same lieu and is there at the present time. There are three flaws in this conclusion: (i) I don't know where the place is; (ii) I don't know why she returned there; (iii) I don't know why she went there in the first place.

Of course he knew! And he'd find her today! Fuck all! There was just one single piece missing. He leaned against a tree and bit his fingernails. All right, all right. It would come. She and Kenny had gone to the motel on Monterey Bay. Okay. And before that? She'd slept in a hotel in Fresno. And before that? Selma, Harford, Coalinga, and

Paso Robles; one night in Santa Maria; LA and Vegas. Could she have gone back to Las Vegas? His radar spun and hummed. No, there was nothing there. LA, then? The radar rasped—zzzzzzzz! Yeah! There was something there! What? They'd landed in Los Angeles. There had been a riot at the airport. She'd injured her arm. A doctor bandaged her. She'd gone to the garage to check out her MG and she'd driven north along the coast. . . . The zzzzzzzz faded. His thoughts scattered.

He stood there blankly.

It was worse than Crossword Number Seven.

It stopped raining. The sun came up. People were walking in the park now. A hurdy-gurdy was playing "Oh! Susannah."

> It rained all night the day I left
> The weather it was dry
> The sun so hot I froze to death
> Susannah don't you cry . . .

Then the mockingbird sang. It sat on a branch just above him, screeching with derision.

He listened to the chiding, delighted. There it was! Jesus God! The mockingbird! Holy Moses! He'd driven into that back road by the golf course; he'd tried to do a crossword puzzle, but that fucking bird had clamored at him like a bugle; a golfer had come over and said, "You can't park here." And she was—having her bandage changed! *Hospitaler!* Hospital! A clinic! On the other side of Fresno! And that's where she was now, by Christ!

Four hours later he was in Fresno. He crossed the city and turned south on the Selma road. He rolled into the side lane bordering the golf course. He climbed out from behind the wheel numbly. He stood there beside the VW for five minutes, licking his lips and trembling like an epileptic. The last eighty miles had almost convinced him that the whole premise was pure wishful thinking, based on total nothingness.

"You can't park there, man." A fat caddie was standing on the other side of the fence, twirling a keychain.

The Eye nodded dumbly and walked up the road to the

gate of the clinic. He stared at the sign on the post. San Joaquin Maternity.

J.

He went into the driveway. Several cars were parked under the trees of a patio. Two Jags, a Mercedes, a Lancia HPE, an Austin Allegro, a Plymouth Volare. And an MG.

The reception room was a wide, low-ceilinged, cool, tiled cave with an imitation Utrillo mural filling a back wall. A pretty girl in a striped uniform was sitting at a desk reading Buster Crabbe's *Energistics*.

"You're too late," she said. He gaped at her. "Visiting hours are from nine thirty till ten thirty. And from two till four." She had a Massachusetts accent and green fingernails.

"Ehhhh . . ." he said. He couldn't speak! His fucking voice was gone! He tightened his lips, concentrated on the Utrillo. A brown windmill. Fences. Trees. A pale blue sky. "I really don't have time for a visit. I was just driving by, and I thought I'd stop and—" Shit! What name was she using? "—and see how our patient was coming along." Charlotte Vincent? Leonor Shelley? Diane Morrell? Mrs. Ralph Forbes? No. She wouldn't want her child born with an alias. Would she?

The girl flipped open the lid of a box of index cards. "What name?"

"Joanna Eris."

"Oh, she's doing fine. Are you a relative?"

"Just a friend, just a friend," he babbled. "I've been away. I came back this morning and heard about—about it. And came right over." He hid his shaking hands in his pockets. "Thought I'd just zip in and—" He swallowed and gulped. "Haven't seen her for a while, and . . ."

"You know"—a whisper—"she lost the baby? A terrible shame. A little girl. But Mrs. Eris is great now. She'll be out of here in a few days."

He gazed at her and saw three girls in striped uniforms sitting at three desks. "I want to see her," he said.

"You better wait until this afternoon. She's under sedation this morning, and—"

"I want to see her."

"But—"

"I want to see her. Please."

"Can't you come back this afternoon?"

"Please."

A nurse came by the desk. The girl got up and followed her. They whispered together, glancing at him. Then the nurse beckoned and led him through the reception room into a passageway.

She opened a door, stepped aside.

The blinds were closed. A single fine clean blade of white sunlight fell across the dark room on Joanna's arm hanging from the bed.

He stood over her.

She was sound asleep, lying on her side, her profile on the pillow an ebon false face of shadows. He sat beside her, his hand reaching out timidly, hovering over her.

He smiled, an enormous quietude settling on his soul. He took her gently by the wrist and lifted her arm to the bed, placing it on the sheet as if it were a fragile shell of jade.

She stirred, her lips parted. She smelled of medicine and balm. Her hair had grown. Her long hands were lank.

He had found her. In recompense for all his loss he had been given this prize—a girl asleep in a dim room. All the world was an abyss filled with her slaughtered men, but she was his redemption and his grace. She had called to him and he had come. He would never leave her now. They would remain forever under the oak trees, with their lost daughters and their miracle.

Eleven

"Who was he?" Joanna asked.

"He didn't give his name," the nurse said.

"And he asked for me?"

"Yes."

"He asked for Joanna Eris?"

"Yes. He said he was a friend of yours."

"What did he look like?"

They were in the clinic garden, walking along a sunken pathway through banks of high grass. The Eye stood less than five feet away from them, concealed on a knoll of lilacs.

"They often do that," the nurse said.

"Who? Do what?"

"Salesmen and photographers and such. They get the names of our patients from the register and then come in here pretending they're members of the family."

"But why?"

"To sell their junk. You know, silverware and baby pictures and all that motherhood shit. Or maybe he was a reporter. They're always sneaking around, too, looking for celebrities having abortions." She named three Hollywood actresses. "They were all at St. Joaq's. Using false names, of course."

"That must be it—yes. Something like that. Nobody knows I'm here." But she wasn't satisfied. She turned and stood with her hands on her hips, peering around the garden.

* * *

The little girl's name was Jessica. She was buried on the banks of the San Joaquin River. Joanna spent an hour there every day, sitting beside the grave over the small headstone bearing the inscription *Jessica Eris 15 days old.*

The cemetery was a woodland, shaded with groves of old trees, filled with slopes of wildflowers, winding walks and hedges and ferns and mossy walls. Joanna would bring jars of roses or tulips or daffodils, place them on the tiny mound, then sit on the ground with her hands folded on her lap and try to come to terms with her grief. The Eye didn't pity her yet. She was stupefied with misery, in a twilight coma of shock. The horror would come later—much later, with the return of perception.

The following weekend she checked out of the clinic and drove to Sacramento. She registered in a hotel as Ellen Tegan, enrolled in a health club and spent three weeks, four hours a day, swimming and exercising. She had her hair cut again. She never drank. She spent some time under a sunlamp and lost her clinic pallor. She took long walks, hundreds of blocks every morning, striding athletically from one end of the city to the other, the Eye trudging behind her.

On one of these killing hikes he became careless and she almost waylaid him. She stopped in a doorway and let him overtake her. He saw the trap at the last minute and, as casually as he could manage it, turned into the nearest building. It was an apartment house. He was in luck; the front door was ajar. He ran through the entranceway into the lobby, stepped into an elevator, and pushed a fifth floor button.

Five minutes later he came back downstairs via the stairway. She was standing in the vestibule, her hands on her hips, reading the names on the mailboxes. He slipped out the back exit, circled the building, and was waiting for her farther up the block when she resumed her walk.

That same afternoon she went to see a man named Pancho Kinski. He had an office in the rear of a yellow brick hovel overlooking an alley. The sign on his door was noncommittal: *Kinski Service.* He was five feet high, wiry and tough, brainless and mean.

He was a private dick.

She hired him for three days for a few bucks an hour, and he came out of his hole and began sleuthing. It didn't take the Eye long to find out what he was up to. He was looking for *him!*

The Eye tried to avoid him but it was impossible—Joanna kept luring him to isolated, out-of-the-way places. A highway diner, a boathouse café on the river, a suburban bowling alley, a little theater in Folsom. And eventually, as inept as he was, Kinski spotted him.

On the third night, he closed in, hard-guy style.

Joanna drove to Lincoln for dinner. The Eye was three miles behind her in the VW Rabbit. A few miles from Roseville a Chevrolet sedan rolled in front of him, forcing him to the side of the road. Pancho jumped out, looking like a tall midget, holding a pistol as big as a piano leg.

"I got you!" he screamed. "Out! Out!"

There were two other creatures with him. A tall scarecrow in a raincoat, aiming a Colt, and another runt wearing a sailor hat and waving a sap.

The Eye didn't like the looks of them, not at all. They were too wild. He obeyed quickly. They searched him, took his .45 away from him.

"You're comin' with us," Pancho snarled. "You hear me? You hear me?"

"I hear you, sure."

"Move! Move it! Move!"

They shoved him into the back of the sedan. The runt got behind the wheel. They drove into Roseville.

"Ike's place," Pancho said.

"Huh?" The runt hit the brakes. The car skidded to a stop, bouncing them.

"What're you stoppin' for? What're you stoppin' for?"

"Huh?" The runt blinked at him, mutton faced.

"Ike's! Ike's! Ike's!"

"Okay, yeah."

They drove on. They were rank with sweat, quaking and jerking with excitement. The three guns—.45, Colt, and cannon—were sticking in the Eye's face. They turned through several back streets, drove twice around the same block.

"Left!" Pancho squealed. "Left! Left!"

"Easy, easy," the scarecrow whispered. "This is the street."

They rolled through an open door into the black pit of a garage, swarmed out of the car, dragging the Eye after them. The runt slid the street door closed, the scarecrow turned on a light. Pancho pushed the Eye against a wall.

"So who are you?" he barked. "Who the fuck are you?"

"Me?"

"You, yeah, you!" He slapped him across the shoulder with the barrel of the cannon. "You!"

"Is this a stickup?"

"What d'you mean is this a stickup? We're legal private investigators workin' legally."

"You abducted me. That's not legal."

"We'll do more than that before we're finished with you, motherfucker!" He barreled him again. "You get the idea?"

"Armed aggression. Fifteen to twenty years."

"You get the idea? I'm askin' you, you get the idea?"

"Show me your license. And your permits to carry all this artillery."

"Belt him, Kinski!" the runt yapped. "Clobber his ass!"

"Why you followin' that little lady for?" Pancho asked.

"What little lady?"

"Miss Tegan. My client. Miss Ellen Tegan."

"I don't know Miss Ellen Tegan."

"Why you followin' her for? Why you followin' her for?"

"I don't even know her. This must be some kind of a screw-up."

"She seen you! She seen your Rabbit! She seen you in Auburn and Folsom! Before that you was shadowin' her in Fresno!"

"I'm not shadowing anybody." He turned to the two clowns. "Abduction. A snatch. Thirty years. Fifty years. Life." But they couldn't hear him. They were having too much fun to listen to points of order.

"Break his arm, Kinski," the runt said.

"I want some answers!" Pancho shouted.

"Cool it down, Pancho," the scarecrow whispered. "You're makin' too much noise."

"Answers! Empty your pockets!"

"You're supposed to call her, Pancho," the scarecrow whispered.

"What?"

"You said you'd call her."

"Yeah. Watch him!" Pancho went over to a phone on the wall, reached up, lifted down the receiver, dialed.

"Break a few bones," the runt grunted, swishing the sap at the Eye.

"Miss Tegan," Pancho yarred into the phone. "Ellen Tegan . . . is she there? Is Miss Tegan there? Well, she'll be in later on because she's got a reservation at your establishment tonight, so tell her to call . . . Hello! hello! Are you listening to me, jackass? Hello! Tell her to call Pancho Kinski . . . Kinski . . . Kinski . . . *K-I-N-S-K-I!* At this number. It's a Roseville number." He gave the number. "You got that? It's a Roseville number. You got it? . . . Right." He hung up.

"I'm goin' keep his piece," the runt said, taking the Eye's .45 away from the scarecrow.

"Give me that," Pancho growled, grabbing for the gun. The runt skipped away from him. "Gimme it! Gimme it!"

The Eye walked over to the light switch and clicked it off. Then he dropped to the floor and rolled under the sedan. The three guns fired a salvo into the blackness. Bullets ricocheted off the walls, the car, the ceiling. The garage buzzed and hummed like a beehive. The windshield collapsed. A tire hissed air. The scarecrow screamed.

The telephone rang.

The Eye got up, turned on the light. They were toppled all over the red floor. The side of the runt's head was nearly sawed off. The scarecrow was kneeling, holding his bleeding stomach, chirruping. There was a bullet hole in Pancho's cheek. The Eye took the .45 away from the runt, pocketed it. He went to the phone, dropped his handkerchief over the receiver, lifted it, then hung up—then lifted it again and let it dangle.

There was a door in the back wall. He came out of the garage into a yard filled with tubs and oil drums and fenders. Voices were shouting in the street. He climbed over a fence, jumped down into a lot, stamping his feet in the dirt to wipe the blood from the bottoms of his shoes. He ran across a dark field of rubble to an adjacent avenue and walked down the block, watching the stars, navigating toward the south.

Two drunks were arguing in front of a bar. A cop came cantering up the sidewalk toward him. The Eye went over to the drunks and tried to separate them. "Come on, fellows," he pleaded. "Let's all be friends."

One of them shoved him away. "Mind your own fuckin' business! This is a grudge fight!"

"He's got it comin' to him!" the other yelled.

"Break it up!" the cop shouted as he raced past them. The Eye walked on. A half-hour later he was out of Roseville on the open road. A Ford convertible filled with hooting youngsters zoomed by. One of them threw a bottle at him. He passed a horse grazing like a silver ghost in a moonlit pasture.

No . . . Joanna didn't know he existed. Not really. No. She was suspicious of everybody and he was just another goblin in her mind. So there were two possibilities: (1) She wanted to disappear again and had hired Kinski to ambush anyone who might be after her. Which meant that she was probably already on the run. (2) She was curious to find out once and for all whether or not she was actually being followed. Which meant that she would stay around awhile to see what Kinski dragged up; which meant that she was in danger now, if the local fuzz found out she was Kinski's client; which meant that she would have to be warned.

He found the Rabbit parked where he'd left it on the shoulder of the road. He climbed behind the wheel and drove to Sacramento.

The MG was in the parking lot behind the hotel. He went to a bar and phoned her room.

"Miss Ellen Tegan?"

"Yes."

Her voice jolted him. "H-hello."

"Hello . . ."

"This is Lieutenant McElligott, State Police. We're investigating the slaying of a Pancho Kinski, and we found your name in his office files . . ."

"Oh, yes. I hired him a couple of days ago to—to find a—something I lost. Slaying, you say?"

"Could you come to my office sometime tomorrow, Miss Tegan? It's just a formality. Make a statement."

"Certainly."

"Thank you. Good night."

"Good night, Lieutenant."

Ten minutes later she checked out of the hotel. She drove to Oakland at a steady eighty MPH.

She spent the rest of the night in a motel, registered as Miss Valerie Anderson. In the morning she sold the MG at a used car lot in Alameda. The Eye got rid of the Rabbit there, too.

She took a taxi to the airport and flew to Boise, Idaho.

She spent two months in Sun Valley. Her new name was Ella Dory.

Mornings and afternoons the Eye, bundled in a fur anorak and scarf, sat shivering on the hotel terrace with his binoculars, watching her ski; nights, he would go to The Igloo, one of the resort taverns, and watch her dance. She became friendly with only one man. And their meeting almost cost the Eye an attack of apoplexy.

As he was coming into The Igloo one evening, she suddenly appeared in front of him, emerging from the tap room.

"I wish you'd stop following me," she said. "Really."

He stood there, petrified.

But she was looking past him at someone standing in the entrance. He turned, saw a slim, dark, smiling man in his fifties, wearing a sheepskin jacket.

"I'm not following you," he laughed. "We just always seem to be going in the same direction at the same time."

The Eye ran outside and gulped down lungfuls of air. He felt as if he'd just tobogganed down the side of Borah Peak.

His name was Jerome Vight. He was an attorney from Little Rock, Arkansas. A bachelor. After that they and several other couples formed a casual skiing and cocktail clique, Joanna completely indifferent to the whole arrangement, and Vight (the Eye watching every phase of his beguilement) becoming more and more captivated by her unconcern. By the end of the first month he was hooked.

Cora Earl was another matter altogether. She was a fashion designer from New York, thirty-two years old, twice divorced, thoroughly misanthropic. She arrived at the hotel one afternoon with a safari of bellboys carrying fifteen pieces of luggage. She saw Joanna sitting in the lounge, marched over to her, and said exactly the right thing.

"I'll bet you a thousand bucks that you've been seduced by at least one of these scurvy ski-bum bastards since you've been here."

Joanna looked at her coolly and held out her hand. "Give me the thousand," she replied.

Cora opened her purse, took out two five hundreds. "I'm in one seventeen C," she said. "Whenever you get horny, come up and sleep with me."

A week later Joanna accepted the offer.

The Eye, watching them dance together in The Igloo, was secretly pleased. She needed someone to restore her self-confidence and to mend her body. No man on earth was capable of the job but Cora was perfect—just as Dr. Martine Darras had been, years ago. Both women were the same opiate of appeasement, the same dream of passion in the night, the same goddess smiling in the tempest, reaching out with a soothing hand to heal a scared hurt.

He followed them back to the hotel. On the seventh-floor corridor he climbed out a window and inched his way along a slippery ledge to the terrace of 117C. He stood in the snow at the window of the suite, watching them.

Joanna was hanging her mink coat over the back of a chair. Then she sat down and pulled off her boots. Cora walked across the room, waving her arms angrily.

". . . I taught her everything she knows about designing clothes, the bitch! In fact, all that LA stuff last year was my idea originally. The harem trousers and the handkerchief bit and jump suits and chamois bathing suits and all that. I called her up last week and said, 'Darling, bravo!' and she said, 'Go fuck yourself!' How do you like that!" She laughed. "But wait'll she sees my new collection! It'll make her rags look like the latest thing from Bulgaria! The little toad!"

She was wearing a deerskin skirt and a see-through chiffon blouson. A cylinder hung on a chain around her neck. Joanna took it in her hand. "What's this?" she asked.

Cora opened it and pulled out a toothbrush. "It's for wherever you happen to be," she said, "afterwards." She peeled everything off and walked naked to the window. Joanna pulled off her sweater and ski suit. She got up, came behind her, leaned against her back. They were standing in the steamy pane just in front of the Eye. Cora touched the glass with her nipples. "What's with you and Jerry Vight?" she whispered.

"He's a Taurus," Joanna said.

Cora reached behind her, put her hands on her hips and pulled her closer. "You ought to grab him. He doesn't know what to do with all his fucking money. But don't put out until he's ready to marry you. I like you on my back." She closed her eyes. "You feel menacing. A friend of mine got sodomized by a cop in Central Park. Said it was heaven! I never tried it. It's supposed to blow all sorts of fuses. Physically, he's repugnant—Jerry, I mean. A weasel. Probably got a cock on him like an obelisk. But he's so fucking rich! He once flew around the world with a girl he picked up in New Orleans. They went to Madrid, Athens, Nairobi, Sydney, Tokyo. Just like that! But I digress!" She turned and took her in her arms. "Let me look at you." She kissed her shoulder. "'To have, to hold,'" she crooned, "'for just one brief hour of ecstasy . . .'"

"My father went to Nairobi," Joanna said. "He was an anthropologist. He wrote a book, *The Beginning of Time*."

"'And then to let you go again,'" Cora sang. Her hands moved between them.

"He went to Mozambique." Joanna lifted her crooked finger to her mouth, bit it. "And sailed up the Crocodile River in a schooner all the way to . . . I don't know where. He never came back. He was looking for the lost tribe of the Limpopo People. The Limpopos were a race of gods who built golden cities all over Africa, aeons ago. They probably never existed . . . but he was certain they were still there, somewhere beyond the rain forests and the plains, living in golden temples, waiting for him. Maybe he found them. Maybe he's there now."

"What the fuck are you talking about?" Cora pulled her down to the floor and wrapped her in her legs.

The Eye climbed over the railing, slid back along the ledge to the corridor window. He went to his room and did a crossword puzzle.

*   *   *

Joanna met Jerry Vight in the coffee shop the next morning. Naturally, he was peeved.

"Let me give you a word of fatherly advice, Ella," he snapped.

" 'Be thy intents wicked or charitable?' " she asked him gravely. " 'Thou com'st in such a questionable shape that I will speak to thee.' "

He scowled. "What?"

"*Hamlet*," she smiled. "What's on your mind, pal?"

"Well, listen . . ." He lowered his voice. "I know this girl-to-girl business is quite the thing these days, and I don't want to sound like an out-of-date fogey, but . . ." He took her by the hand. "Cora is a whore. A genuine honest-to-God creep, Ella. She's selfish, cruel, egomaniacal, and completely heartless. When she's through with you she'll just kick you out and slam the door."

Joanna laughed. "You make her sound like a man."

"She's worse than a man," he said. "She's neuter."

The Eye, sitting at a nearby table, watched Joanna's face. Her wanness had vanished overnight. She was wearing her killer's mask again. He felt cold fists of stage fright grip his vitals.

She struck on New Year's Eve.

As soon as the sun went down, he climbed out the corridor window to the terrace of 117C. He'd been doing this every night for the last three weeks and was now familiar with every slippery foot of the ledge and the cornice.

It was snowing.

He stood in the white darkness, staring through the window. She was alone, lying on the floor, nude. Her back was covered with nail scratches and bruises. She sat up, held out her arms. They were wrapped from wrists to shoulders in shimmering garlands of bracelets. A string of pearls was tied around her waist. One of Cora's fifteen pieces of luggage was open before her. It was a small blue leather case filled with jewelry. She took a diamond ring and slipped it on her little toe. She turned and smiled. He could see her liquid green eyes all the way across the room, shining with pleasure as she pinned a small ruby on her ear. She was almost looking at him, and it was as if his presence were the cause of her delight.

He raised his hand, waved at her timidly.

She rolled over on her spine like a cat and scratched her back on the rug. Then she jumped up, took her watch from the chimney, checked the time. She put all the jewels back in the case, closed and locked the lid.

She went into the bedroom. She reappeared, dragging Cora's naked, rigid body by the feet. She pulled it across the room, opened the window. The Eye climbed up on the ledge and hid in a black angle of the wall. Joanna lifted the corpse and pitched it over the railing. It dropped down seven stories into the cul-de-sac alleyway behind the hotel and sank into nine feet of snow. She went back into the room and closed the window.

Fifteen minutes later the Eye was down in the lobby, checking out. At nine o'clock she emerged from the elevator, followed by a bellboy carrying her luggage. She was holding the blue leather jewel case under her arm, wrapped in her mink. She paid her bill, then sent the boy off looking for Vight. She sat down in the lounge and lit a Gitane.

There was a party in the bar. An orchestra was playing beer hall polkas. Guests in paper hats were reeling in and out of all the passages, throwing streamers and blowing whistles.

Jerry came across the lounge, his dinner jacket sprinkled with confetti.

"What is it, Ella?"

"You were right." She held a handkerchief to her eyes, sniffed and whimpered. "She gave me my walking papers. It was awful. I feel so shitty. You should have heard her. You were right. She's a monster."

"Well . . ." He didn't know what to say. "The hell with her."

She got up. "So long, Jerry."

"What do you mean so long?"

"I'm leaving." She went out into the lobby.

He followed her. "Ella! Wait a second . . . Ella! . . . Please—listen to me! You can't—Ella! . . ."

He checked out, too.

They were married that night in Boise. They flew to Honolulu the next morning.

Twelve

The Eye sat on the beach behind the gutted hull of a row-boat, watching them through his binoculars. He was on the point of a *W* between two coves. The Cariddi was anchored in the inlet to the left, a quarter of a mile offshore. Jerry was squatting on the forward deck, wearing a straw hat and drinking a can of orange juice.

They'd been coming out here every afternoon for the last three days, looking for the American destroyer that was supposed to be down there somewhere on the bottom of Kaneoke Bay.

Joanna surfaced, climbed up the ladder. She was naked to the waist, wearing a pair of jeans cut off at the thigh. She pushed the mask onto the top of her head, sat down on the bow. "Christ! The water's like oil. What's the temperature?"

"Ninety-seven."

Their voices carried across the cove with amphitheatre clearness. The Eye could even hear the hum of the radio in the cabin.

"It's twenty below in Boston. And it's snowing in New Orleans."

"Turn off the goddamned radio," she said.

"I want to hear the news."

"What for?"

"My! You look fetching!" He tried to crawl between her knees. She laughed, kicked him away.

The laugh was false—almost hysterical. Jerry couldn't

interpret it, but the Eye, who knew her much better than he did, was perfectly aware of what it meant. She was in mortal danger, so tautly drawn that she was giddy with tension. Every hour brought her closer to disaster. Five whole days had passed, and Cora's body hadn't been found yet. But perhaps at this very moment they were shoveling it out of the snow, and this evening the hunt for Ella Dory would begin. She wouldn't be difficult to locate. Her spoor led directly from Idaho to Oahu—directly to this blue cove in the warm sea. And instead of fleeing, she was forced to linger here in the sun, playing vacation games and parrying the amorous gropings of a man she loathed.

"There's no destroyer." Jerry threw the can overboard.

"There's something down there."

"Where?"

"Just behind all those fucking weeds. A great big bump covered with sand."

"No kidding!"

"As big as a house."

This morning, while Jerry was having breakfast, she'd gone out and bought a pair of handcuffs in a toy shop near the hotel. The Eye had watched.

Jerry tossed his straw hat onto the roof of the cabin. "Let's have a look." He donned his mask and flaps and jumped off the deck. Joanna sat there a moment, staring at the beach. Then she got up and pulled off her jeans, opened her bag, took out the handcuffs, unlocked their prongs. And over the side she went.

Flies devoured the Eye. He slapped his arms and neck, the blows echoing like rifle shots up and down the beach. The stink of salt and warm rot almost suffocated him. A spiked fin floated into the cove. He watched it dully, measuring it. It looked like a long golf bag drifting in the current. He jumped up. Shit! It was a motherfucking shark! It circled the Cariddi, swam into the surf, thrashed atop a breaker. Jesus! It was gigantic! It twisted, dived. Joanna came up the ladder, her buttocks twinkling in the sun. The Eye crawled behind the rowboat, lifted his binoculars. She jumped over the cabin, unhooked the anchor chain from the aft cleat, dropped it overboard. The shark surfaced, bumped against the stern, dived again. Joanna went to the helm, started the engine. The Cariddi groaned and turned toward the open sea.

The Eye sat there a moment, watching it round the right headland of the *W*. Then he looked at the water. The cove was a mire of blue and green. Jerry was still down there, handcuffed to the anchor.

With the shark.

The Eye had already checked out and was sitting in the lobby doing a crossword puzzle when she arrived. She was wearing sandals and a sleeveless turquoise beach tunic. Her emerald eyes, overflowing in her sun-blackened face, were almost unbearably exotic. She looked about eighteen years old.

The waiting was over. She was on the run now, cool and smooth.

"Mr. Vight has gone to Lahaina," she told the clerk. "He'll be back on Friday or Saturday."

"Yes, Mrs. Vight."

"Get me a reservation on a flight to San Francisco this afternoon."

"Are you leaving us?"

"Just for a week. My mother is ill."

"Oh, I'm sorry to hear that!"

"Nothing serious. She sprained her wrist playing tennis or something."

The Eye found a copy of yesterday's *Los Angeles Herald-Examiner* on the plane. Cora Earl's picture was on page one, under the headline *SUSPICIOUS FALL IN SUN VALLEY! Inquest to Decide Cause of Celebrated Designer's Death.*

That night she stayed at the Mark Hopkins and kept her Mrs. Ella Vight alias until she'd cashed all of Jerry's traveler's checks. Then, wearing a red wig and changing her identity, she sold Cora's jewels to a fence in San Mateo for another heavy bundle. She put nearly sixty thousand dollars in a safe-deposit box in a bank in Oakland the next day before leaving for the airport.

The Eye tried to get a seat on the same flight to Mexico City, but there were no vacancies. He tried two other airlines. All the Thursday planes were booked; the standby lists were filled. The catastrophe was so unexpected that he didn't even have time to panic. Her flight was announced, she walked into the boarding ramp, stopped, glanced once over her shoulder, and was gone. By the time he realized he'd probably never see her again, she was airborne.

Shit. From Mexico she could vanish in any direction—South America, the Caribbean, Europe—no, she couldn't! *She couldn't get a passport.* So it wasn't total finality. She'd be only twelve hours ahead of him. And she'd probably stay overnight, at least—right? Maybe a day or two. Plenty of time. He made a reservation for the earliest Friday morning flight. Besides, there was still the safe-deposit box in Oakland. He could stake out the bank. She'd go back there sooner or later—in a month, six months, a year. His heart sank. A year? Shit.

He took a taxi back to the Mark Hopkins. He'd go to a movie, have dinner, get to bed early. His radar whined. In the lobby two men were standing at the desk, talking to the clerk. They were both young, long-haired, fit, wearing natty overcoats with fur collars. Feds!

"Mrs. Vight? Yes—" The clerk was rattled. "She checked out two hours ago."

"Any idea where she was going?" Number One asked.

"No, sir. She just paid her bill and—"

"Describe her," Number Two cut in.

"In her twenties—late twenties, I guess. Sunburned. Short hair. Blue eyes. Tall, about five eleven . . ."

"Fine," Number One nodded. "That's an excellent description. And you don't know where she is now?"

"Mrs. Vight?" The Eye, all smiles, moved closer. "She's in Denver."

They stared at him. "You know her?" Number Two asked.

"Know her? Gosh, no. Wish I did. Lovely girl. We just had a friendly drink together last night. Matter of fact, I invited her to dinner, but she had a previous engagement, I'm sorry to say."

He tried not to overdo it. They'd already sized him up—clothes, accent, fingernails, haircut—and classified him as a Type O: out-of-town oaf. A midwestern or New England bumpkin, Honest Homer Hayseed.

"And she told you she was going to Denver?"

"Yup." He smacked his lips smugly. "I can even give you her address."

"We'd appreciate it."

"Ramada Inn."

"Ramada Inn, Denver. Check."

"Said she'd be stayin' there a couple of weeks, then go on to—ahhh . . . Kansas City, I think. No! I take that back. Omaha! Omaha, Nebraska!"

"Much obliged."

"Not at all."

They left. So did he. He went into the coffee shop and slipped out a side exit to the street. The crowd closed around him like a comforting bog of eiderdown. Feds, by Christ! From Sun Valley or Honolulu? For the next forty-eight hours all of Colorado and Nebraska was going to be Dragnetville! That would keep the motherfuckers busy for a while. But then they'd start backtracking.

He went into the bar and had two large cognacs. Then he checked into the Sir Francis Drake. He couldn't sleep. He sat up all night reading *Helter Skelter*. He was at the airport at seven thirty. The plane took off at eight ten.

He found her at a quarter to twelve. She was sitting on a bench on the Paeseo de la Reforma, eating a pear.

It was as if she were waiting for him—except that there was a man with her.

"Why are you smiling?" he asked.

"I don't know," she laughed. "For some reason or other, I feel—all of a sudden—I feel blissful. Reprieved."

"Reprieved?"

"As if I were going to the gas chamber this morning, at"—she glanced at her watch—"eleven forty-five exactly. And the warden just walked into my cell and said, 'Miss Kane, let me be the first to congratulate you. You have been reprieved.' And I take a deep breath, and instead of inhaling cyanide, I smell the trees in the park and the water in the lake. And the flower stalls and the fruit carts."

"Are you sure you're not sniffing glue, too?"

"Let's go to church and light candles."

"I'd rather go to San Juan Ixtayoapan and have a look at that new supermarket complex."

His name was Rex Hollander. He was an architect from Savannah. He was forty-eight years old, recently divorced, lonely, cheerful, and boyish. He'd just built a seven-million-dollar office building in Mazatlán.

They spent the next three weeks together, visiting Atzcaptzalco, Ixtacalco, Coyoacán and the usual tourist places, returning to the city every evening for the restaurants and the nightlife. They lived in separate suites at the hotel and weren't sleeping together yet. They played tennis and golf, they swam and went to the bullfights. They joined a private gambling club and Joanna lost four thousand dollars at chemin de fer. They took one long, grueling train trip to Juchitán and Tonala to look at some new apartment buildings.

Joanna was happy and at peace—her laughter was genuine, and apparently she had no intention of murdering him, at least for a while. The Eye did crossword puzzles in Spanish. He read *The Conquest of Mexico* by William H. Prescott. He bought a shawl for Maggie.

On January the thirtieth two divers found an arm handcuffed to an anchor chain on the bottom of Kaneoke Bay. On February the second Rex Hollander was on the cover of *Time*: "The Dissident Builder—A Challenge to Urbanization." To celebrate, he and Joanna went to bed together. The next day they flew to Tucson, Arizona. On February the fifth a justice of the peace married them in Casa Grande.

They rented a station wagon and trailer in Phoenix and drove north on a camping trip to Grand Canyon Park. On February the sixth the Hawaiian police identified the Kaneoke arm as having belonged to Jerome Vight. On February the seventh the *Los Angeles Times*, in a story on page three, reported that the deaths of Vight in Hawaii and Cora Earl in Sun Valley were "in all probability" connected and that the FBI was seeking a Miss Ella Dory "for questioning."

Ella Dory—AKA Mary Linda Kane, AKA Mrs. Rex Hollander, *née* Joanna Eris—and her husband were wandering across the Coconino Plateau, driving by night, camping during the day to avoid the heat.

The Eye followed them in a rented Mercury, keeping his

distance. When they'd stop, he'd park the car and circle the trailer on foot, like an Apache. Once a large dusty scorpion stung the heel of his shoe, scaring him shitless. Another time he stepped into a hole atop a family of gila monsters. He began to hate Arizona passionately.

One morning Joanna drove into a nearby town, alone, for supplies. When she came back, she hammered the first nail into Rex's coffin.

"Rex, I just phoned my broker in LA. I'm in a jam."

"What's the problem, dandelion?"

"I need forty thousand dollars before the market closes on Friday. Can you loan it to me?"

"Sure thing!" He wrote out a check. She put it in an envelope, then drove back to town and pretended to mail it. She bought a rifle.

That same afternoon, all hell broke loose.

The Eye, prowling through a moonscape of crags, came upon the carcass of a jackal. Huge fat red ants were devouring it. Farther on, sticking out of a gulch, was a tin sign: Devil's Mesa, Population 15. There was nothing else there except part of a fence and the ruins of a mud hut. And a rattlesnake. It reared up out of the stones, glaring at him. He jumped back, tripped and fell, rolled ass over head down a gully.

Rex saw him. He sprang out of the trailer, wild with excitement. "Mary Lin! There's a guy up there in the rocks!"

She laughed. "No there isn't. That's just my poltergeist."

"Your which?"

"A spirit I invented to haunt myself. Pay no attention to him."

"Like hell! Give me your rifle!"

"Rex, I won't have you gunning down my spirit."

"Then let's capture the sonofabitch alive! You cut around there behind him. I'll go straight up the hill."

The Eye crawled into an escarpment of boulders, cursing him, cursing himself. He hid in a cleft, praying nothing would come out of the ground to gnaw on him.

Rex came up the slope, ran past him, moved across the gulch behind the hut. Then Joanna appeared, coming from the opposite direction. She stopped, stood for a moment staring at the ants. She looked at the sign, walked past the fence into Devil's Mesa.

The rattler rolled out of its lair, coiled on the trail in front of her. She froze. "Hi," she whispered. Its head bobbed toward her, its jaws opening and hissing. The Eye pulled his .45 from his belt. But she was in no danger—not yet. She had time enough to retreat. But she didn't move. She just stood there, waiting. The snake swayed closer, rattling angrily. Rex came around the side of the hut.

"Did you see him?" he called.

"No."

"I guess we scared him off." He walked toward her. "Look at this godforsaken place. It's like a John Ford movie."

Joanna's arms came up slowly. "It must have been a ranch or something," she said, and oh-so-slowly put her hands on her hips, relaxed.

"Imagine anyone living in this inferno!" The snake's head jerked around. The Eye watched them, fascinated. Rex moved closer—closer. His boot kicked a stone, the butt of the rifle scraped along the ground. Closer. Joanna remained motionless. Closer.

"It's perfect for sunbaths." She forced a laugh.

"What a place to spend a honeymoon!" He reached for her. "Let's go back down to the trailer and—"

His shadow fell across the snake. The rattle snapped like a castanet. The jaws flew into the air, struck him on the crotch. He screamed, dropped the rifle. He hobbled back. "Mary Lin!" The jaws hit him again, on the stomach. "Mary Lin!"

Then the Eye heard the car.

He came out of the cleft, climbed over the boulders to the top of the ridge. A sheriff's cruiser was driving along the narrow trail behind the escarpment.

"Mary Lin!"

He ran down to the gulch. The snake was gone. So was Joanna. Rex was sitting on the ground, bellowing. He turned, saw the Eye. He tried to pull himself to his feet. "I can't move my hips!" he howled. "I'm paralyzed! I can't move my hips!"

The Eye picked up Joanna's rifle, ran back to the summit of the ridge. The cruiser pulled into a gully just below him. The doors opened. A fat sheriff in a Stetson squeezed out from behind the wheel. Two men alighted from the other side—the same two Feds he'd met in the lobby of the Mark Hopkins last month. They stood listening to Rex's shrieks echoing through the canyons around them.

"Sounds like a fucking panther!"

The Eye dropped to one knee and fired. The first two bullets punctured the cruiser's front and rear tires, the third slammed through the open door and pulverized the dashboard radio. The three men scattered for cover in the rocks.

He slid down the boulders and ran around the rim of the gulch to the slope above the camp. Joanna was in the station wagon, driving toward the road.

He glanced over at Rex. He was lying on his back in the dust, still calling to her. "Mary Lin!" His face was covered with gurgling froth, his fists were beating his abdomen. "Mary Lin!"

The Mercury was parked a quarter of a mile to the south. The Eye raced toward it. A bullet dropped out of nowhere and tapped him on the shoulder. He thought it was the snake and yelled with terror. His feet kicked in opposite directions. He found himself surging through the air like a high jumper.

"Halt, you cocksucker!" a voice shouted.

He landed on his side in a deep rug of sand, all his bones dislocated. He reached behind him, tried to grasp the rattler's head. He touched the wound and brayed.

"Halt!"

A ricochet bounced past him.

"Halt!"

He rolled behind a dune. He looked at his left arm. It was still there. He lifted it, flapped it, flexed his fingers. Fibers of exquisite pain twanged up and down his back, almost lulling him to sleep. Fuck all! He was going to pass out! He got up, stumbled toward the Mercury. He opened the door—oops! The plateau tilted, flipping him behind the wheel. He started the motor. So far, so good! All he had to do now was keep moving. They'd never catch him, not

without tires or a radio. Butterflies fluttered past the windshield—bright clouds of them, yellow and orange and
black-dotted and gaudy.

Maggie reached over and closed the door. She opened
the valise, took out the Mexican shawl. She wrapped it
around him, pulled it tight. Good, okay. The bleeding
stopped. Thanks. She pointed to the speedometer. He was
doing fifty. He slowed to twenty. She showed him where
the road was, held the wheel, steered him out of the rocks.
Right. He was on the road. Fine. He accelerated. Thirty
. . . forty . . . fifty . . . sixty . . . whoopee!

She turned on the air-conditioner. She wiped his cheeks
with her cool fingers. He wondered what she looked like.
She leaned on him, wedging him against the door so he
wouldn't topple over. When the sun went down, she
switched on the lights. Thanks. Then she turned on the
radio. In the close darkness he could feel her breathing. He
was afraid to move his head . . . his neck was too stiff
. . . he'd look at her in a moment, though . . . he had
to. . . . She poked him awake when he fell asleep. Thanks.
She sang to him.

> It won't be a stylish marriage
> I can't afford a carriage
> But you'll look sweet
> Upon the seat
> Of a bicycle built for two . . .

The station wagon was a mile ahead of them.

Thirteen

Nine hours later, at three o'clock in the morning, they were in Albuquerque. The station wagon turned into a motel, putting an end to the grisly journey.

The Mercury skidded into an all-night filling station, knocked over a pile of cans, scraped against a gas pump, and banged into a fence. The Eye sat behind the wheel, chuckling at a disc jockey's joke. " 'Doctor, it's terrible, I'm losing my memory! What'll I do?' And the doctor said, 'Well, first of all, pay me in advance.' " He turned off the radio, opened the door, tried to move his legs.

A girl in overalls came rushing out of the garage. "You fuckhead! What the fuck's all this!" Then she saw the bloody shawl and whistled.

He slid to the ground, leaned against the fender. "Can I have a glass of water?"

"Sure."

"And give the young lady a Coke or something."

"What young lady?"

He squinted at the car. Maggie was gone. "Oh, that's right . . . she got out in Arizona." It was true. She'd left him somewhere in the Petrified Forest. She'd just opened the door and jumped away into the night. He'd seen her once after that, in New Mexico, standing in a field, waving to him . . .

The girl pulled a Smith and Wesson .38 out of her overalls and aimed it at him nonchalantly. "Now," she drawled, "I don't want no part of whatever you're mixed up with."

"Me?" He grinned at her. "I'm not mixed up with anything."

"Cut yourself shavin', maybe?"

"Something like that, yeah." He gave her a fifty and told her to phone the local Watchmen, Inc., number. While he was waiting, he sat down on the curb, wrapped in the shawl like a tired old woman, and drank a quart of water. She kept the .38 pointed at him.

Twenty minutes later an operative named Dace arrived in a red MGB. He was wearing cowboy boots. The Eye waved to him. "Howdy!"

"Can you move, pal?"

"Nope."

Dace picked him up and put him in the car. He drove him to an out-of-the-way house in Istela. A doctor probed the wound with hooks and pulled a ton of pig iron out of his shoulder. The Eye fainted twice. When he woke up, the second time he was bandaged and high on M. The sun was shining.

"So how do you feel?" Dace asked him.

"Keen!" He got up and moved across the floor like a tightrope walker. "Nifty peachy keen." The hole in his back was smothered in numbness. His left arm was weightless. "Just dandy." He touched his chin. "I need a shave."

"Doc says you ought to stay put awhile."

"No way. Can't."

"Your Mercury's outside."

"Can't do it. I have to—my what? The Mercury?" He walked back and forth, the M seeping through him, untying all the knots. "You take care of that for me, will you, Race . . . Mace . . . Pace . . ."

"Dace."

"Get rid of it. I won't need it anymore."

"Are you lucid, pal?"

"I'll be leaving here by plane. You can drive me to the airport in your MG. What do you mean am I lucid?"

"Can you hear me?"

"Certainly I can hear you."

"Good, because I got bad news for you."

"Just park it somewhere where they can find it. How far are we from Albuquerque? Let me put on a clean shirt and you can get me out of here. . . . Bad news?"

"Are you sure I'm getting through to you, pal?"

"Yeah, speak up."

"I've just been talking to **Mr.** Baker on the phone. He says to tell you you're fired. And he wants **you** to give me his Minolta camera."

He checked his luggage at the airport and took a taxi to the motel. She was still there. It was eleven o'clock. She was running late. With the FBI one state behind her she'd have to move faster than that.

He went back to the airport, had a shave in the barbershop, and waited for her in the lounge. She'd be in sooner or later. She had to leave by plane. Keeping the station wagon was out of the question, and renting another car was almost as risky. And she was in too much of a hurry to take a train.

He sat sweating and squirming as the M faded, laying bare his pain. He thought about Watchmen, Inc. They could never fire him if he made an issue of it. Or if he groveled a bit. All he had to do was telephone Baker and promise him he'd be back at the office tomorrow. But why bother? He would never go back now.

Eleven forty-five. Where the fuck was she? For better or for worse. In sickness and in health. He swallowed an aspirin. He wondered who would take over his desk in the corner by the window. It had been his only home for twenty years. Jesus! What had he left in the drawer? A bottle of Old Smuggler, a tube of glue, his sewing kit and razor, pens and pencils. Twenty years!

"Yeah," he said aloud.

She arrived at noon, wearing a red wig. She bought a ticket to Savannah.

What kept you so long! We should have been out of here hours ago!

Do you think Rex is dead?

I don't know. Probably.

If he is, how long will it be before the bank knows about it?

What bank?

His bank, stupid!

A couple of days. They'll notify his family first. Why? You're worried about the check?

Yes. How's your arm?

*Petrified. Listen, you're not going to try to cash that
fucking check, are you, Joanna?*

Of course I am.

He dropped into a rear seat and fell sound asleep. He
walked for hours along the school corridor, looking for the
classrooms. But there were no doors, just walls. He
pounded on them with his left fist until his arm dropped
off. Then, in a dim alcove in the back of the building, he
found a bulletin board. There was a message from Maggie
pinned to it, scribbled on a piece of wrinkled brown wrap-
ping paper.

> *Dear Daddy,*
>
> *Thanks for the postcard. I'm
> sorry I couldn't wait for you.
> I don't like to hang around here
> after school. These corridors are
> haunted by the ghost of a madman
> who beats on the walls. Give my
> regards to Joanna.*
>
> *Sincerely,*
>
> *Mag*

The throbbing in his shoulder subsided, and he knew that
everything was going to be all right.

They landed in Savannah at three thirty. Using her Mrs.
Mary Linda Hollander identity (blond wig), she cashed
Rex's forty-thousand-dollar check at his bank in Port Went-
worth, then, the same night, flew to Miami and checked
into a beach front hotel in Dania, registering as Miss Ada
Larkin (pewter wig).

The Eye moved into a smaller—and cheaper—place a
block from the beach. His wound healed slowly. In March
he could bend his arm behind his back without agony and
by April was doing five push-ups a day.

He telephoned his band and learned that his Watchmen
paychecks had stopped coming in on February the twenty-
eighth. So he was officially retired—and in Florida al-

ready! He prepared a budget and estimated that he could live off his account for at least three years. After that— fuck it! He'd see.

He bought another suit—he now had three—and an old Fiat. He did four or five crossword puzzles a day, and at night he dreamed not only of the corridor but of the rattle snake and the shark. Sometimes, alone in his room or walking along the beach, he found himself whistling "La Paloma."

Joanna AKA Ada Larkin gradually became herself again, eating pears, buying clothes, drinking cognac, and reading her horoscope.

She slept all morning, swam in the afternoon, and gambled every evening. In four weeks she'd almost doubled the forty grand playing roulette. The Eye played for much lower stakes at the blackjack and crap tables, averaging a comfortable profit of about two hundred a night, which paid for his rent and most of his expenses.

One hot noontime he dropped into a bar for a drink, and saw a sign on the wall: TRY PILSEN—The Czechoslovakian Beer. This reminded him that he still hadn't finished Puzzle Number Seven.

He went to the public library and spent an hour reading the history of Czechoslovakia in several encyclopedias and almanacs. It was, he discovered, a totalitarian Communist-bloc people's democracy, but formerly an independent republic, founded after World War I and comprising the former countries of Bohemia, Moravia, Silesia, and Slovakia, each with a capital—a capital *in* Czechoslovakia: Prague, Brünn, Breslau, and Bratislava. Six letters, five letters, seven letters, and ten letters. None of them could be squeezed into *Capital in Czechoslovakia*'s four letters.

He finally decided to look up the solution in the last pages of the paperback. But he didn't.

He went to the beach instead and watched Joanna diving in the surf.

He began getting restless.

She kept too much to herself. That was a mistake. A lone female wandering around Miami was a come-on more blatant than skywriting. People were beginning to notice her and gossip—guests at the hotel, croupiers, bartenders, waiters, bellhops.

I think we have to get moving, Joanna, he warned her.
Not yet.

She bought a new wig (auburn). She went to an oculist and had her eyes examined. She visited the animal veldt in Boca Raton. She went to the movies.

He made a list of the films she saw.

> (April 15) *Klute*
> (April 19) *I heard the Owl Call My Name*
> (April 20) *Jane Eyre*
> (April 21) *Catholics*
> (April 23) *Jane Eyre* (again)
> (April 25) *Dollars*
> (April 27) *Jane Eyre* (again)

He made a list of the magazines she bought.

Vogue	*Newsweek*
Elle	*The New Yorker*
Time	*Cosmopolitan*
Glamour	*Good Housekeeping*
McCall's	*Paris-Match*

He made a list of the books she read.

> *Jane Eyre* by Charlotte Brontë
> *War and Peace* by Tolstoy
> *Nana* by Zola
> *Moby Dick* by Melville
> *The End of the Affair* by Greene
> *Hamlet*

He made a list of her killings.

> Paul Hugo
> Dr. Brice
> Bing Argyle
> Cop in NYC

Cora Earl
Jerome Vight
Rex Hollander

Seven of them that he was sure of. Four husbands.
Come on, Joanna, we have to move on now!
Oh, not yet.

Then, in May, three or four limousines drove up to the hotel and a swarm of Arabs took over all the top-floor suites. There was an item about them in the paper that morning: *Arab Delegation in Town for Real Estate Talks*.
When the Eye saw them in the lobby, he almost fell through the floor. One of them was Abdel Idfa!
Jesus Christ!

For the rest of the afternoon the playful elves of impending doom took over the situation.
They made Joanna pick that very day of days to change her schedule. Instead of going to the beach she went out to the pool and practiced diving for an hour. Abdel Idfa joined her there, as if by appointment, and lay sprawled in a deck chair sunbathing less than twenty feet away from her.
Then they both spent a half-hour in the patio cocktail lounge, drinking martinis, entering one behind the other, each sipping two drinks at opposite ends of the bar, then leaving together so simultaneously that they almost collided at the door.
The Eye went berserk with funk. The crowds saved her! Thank God for all these vacationing walk-ons, these Beautiful Miami People—the athletic Tarzans in Ted Lapidus jockstraps and the innumerable undressed chicks darting around and the purple-haired old women in giant sunglasses and their beefsteak-faced husbands wearing Bermuda shorts! They were everywhere, vast gaggles of them, encompassing everything in moats and ramparts of noise and movement and denseness.
Then, at two o'clock on the dot, they both had lunch in the hotel dining room, Abdel and several fellow tribesmen at one table, Joanna at another, separated from him only by some potted plants and a few dozen other diners.

Then she spent two hours reading in her room, and he went off somewhere. But, lo and behold, they both met again in the lobby at four thirty, she coming out of the elevator, he emerging from the barbershop. They passed each other just in front of the desk, a few centimeters apart, she tossing her key into the slot, he asking the clerk for some cablegram blanks.

The Eye couldn't take any more.

He went to a florist shop on Tampa Street and bought two dozen roses to be delivered to her room. He scribbled a card to go with them.

> Dear Miss Larkin,
> I saw you in the swimming pool this
> afternoon and ever since have been
> wondering if you are the same
> young lady I met in Chicago some time
> ago. But whether you are or
> not, can you join me for a drink?
> I am in 196-197.
>   Abdel Idfa, Esq

She checked out so fast he didn't even have time to sell his Fiat. He left it in the airport parking lot.

She put on her new auburn wig, and they flew to Detroit.

Her name was now Roxane Devorak.

She spent four months in Michigan, living in Lansing, Grand Rapids, and St. Joseph, just across the lake from the Chicago apartment house where she stabbed Bing Argyle.

In September she went to Pittsburgh for a month, then spent two months in Buffalo and another month in Tonawanda, near Niagara Falls, gambling every night in a local clip joint. She lost nine thousand dollars. The Eye won eleven thousand.

One morning he looked out the window and saw that it was snowing.

It was Christmas Eve. Another year had passed.

They flew to Philadelphia and landed in a blizzard.

Fourteen

Wrapped in her mink, Joanna wandered through the streets, window-shopping and listening to the Salvation Army bands playing carols. On the twenty-fourth her horoscope advised her:

> This is YOUR month and 'tis
> the season to be cheerful, so
> take advantage of the jollity
> and try to enjoy yourself . . .

She obeyed the instructions and kept smiling eagerly and fixedly at the passing crowds, as if she were waiting to greet someone amid the merriment. She gave a dollar to a seedy-looking Santa Claus on Market Street. "Thanks," he said, glancing at her legs. "I gotta Xmas present for you too, baby." And he reached down and zipped open his red trousers, showing her his cock wrapped in strings of tinsel.

She went into a department store and roamed up and down the aisles. The loudspeaker was playing "God Rest Ye Merry, Gentlemen." Thousands of people swarmed around her. She bought a sweater. She walked through a forest of giant blinking cardboard Christmas trees. There were children everywhere. She saw scores of Jessicas, clinging to their parents' hands, passing her by, leaving her behind apart from their joy. She was no longer smiling.

The Eye, too, saw his daughter wherever he looked. She was with her real fathers, harried, happy, capable men who

131

held her tightly and gently so she wouldn't go astray in the tumult, and who would guide her home tonight to the warm rooms of comfortable houses with holly on the windows.

He lost sight of Joanna. When he found her again there was a man with her.

He never learned his name, it was all over and done with so quickly.

They wandered along the street and into a cocktail lounge, where they sat together drinking grogs for the rest of the afternoon.

"Yes, I've been dashing all over the country," she said, "for months and months."

"You're lucky to be able to travel," the man replied. "I just don't have the time." He was in his fifties, calm and serious. A good man, obviously, someone who was never cruel or sly.

"But I'd like to rest for a while now." She lit a Gitane, leaned back, looked around the dim room. "Here."

"Why not? Philly's a nice town. I think you'd like it."

"Rent a house and just sleep and . . ." She touched her silver disc. "I'm so weary."

"I could help you to find a house. That's no problem."

"That's no problem, no." She laughed. "The problem is—"

"What?"

Standing just beyond their table was a small Christmas tree. Joanna stared at it. In a corner of the lounge a pianist was playing "Jingle Bells." Frost covered the windows, clouding the light with snowy cumulonimbus grayness.

"The problem is," she said, "what will I do tomorrow? Or the day after that. Or next Christmas." She had begun probably with the intention of telling him some story. But she was meandering now, speaking almost to herself. "How long can I rest? Time passes so quickly. And it's so expensive. It costs a fortune to buy a day or a year from life. We have to pay rent to live in the world. Every time the earth turns the landlord wants his money. And my purse is always empty—I spend all my time and all my money—and I have nothing to show for it. Absolutely nothing. All I possess is a sense of loss. I've lost everything."

"What have you lost?"

They stared at each other. She smiled at him. "Are you a banker?"

"No. What makes you think that?"

"You look like one of those people . . ."

"What people?"

"In a bank, sitting at a desk in a roped-off cubbyhole. Every time I try to cash a check the girl behind the counter goes over and whispers to you and you both look at me. And you pick up a phone and call somebody in another cubbyhole and finally the girl comes back and says, 'Do you have any identification, please?' "

"I'm in advertising."

"No." She shook her head. "No you're not, you're a banker asking me why I have a debit."

"I simply asked you what you lost."

"Well, I'll tell you. I lost my childhood and my youth. My father and my husband. My daughter. And my mind— that's going too now, my memory keeps playing tricks on me. All my thoughts are muddy. And my eyes—" She squinted at him. "I'm becoming myopic. Everything's a blur. I need glasses. What will I do when I'm old and broke and blind and out of my head?"

The pianist was playing "La Paloma." The waiter brought them two more drinks.

"Who requested that number?" she asked him.

"I dunno," he said morosely.

" 'La Paloma,' " she grimaced. "They were playing that the night Daddy left New York. We saw *Hamlet* with Richard Burton. Before that we went—we went ice skating all morning. And in the afternoon we walked up Riverside Drive to Grant's Tomb—a magnificent day. There were huge gray ships with orange smokestacks in the Hudson. The sun was shining. There were lilacs in the park. Who was it who said 'The Earth cannot answer'? It's not true! The Earth can speak. It can sing to you. Trees and streets and lilacs can play music in your ears, if you listen, and if you're a young girl, walking along Riverside Drive with your father. After the theater we went to a party somewhere on the East Side, I think. Everybody thought I was his girl friend, or pretended they did—'I picked her up on Forty-second Street,' he'd say when they kidded him. Then we went to Kennedy and he caught his plane. It had been such a long day, all morning, afternoon, and evening; and we were together every single minute. But it was the last day and the last night. I never saw him again."

"Where did he go?"

"Who knows?"

"What happened to him?"

"He just flew away. He bought me a sweater. It didn't fit. A red sweater. And the loudspeaker was playing 'La Paloma.' They said he had a heart attack. Now, whenever I come out of a bank I pretend he's waiting for me on the corner. But he doesn't need money anymore—it's a shame, because it would be nice to buy things for him. I'd like him to meet my daughter, too. He doesn't even know he's a grandfather. We could all live together in that house you're going to find for me. But of course we can't. They're both dead. And I'm getting drunk."

He didn't laugh or mock her. He didn't reach across the table and take her hand and say. "Let's get out of here and go somewhere else." He couldn't follow all of what she was trying to tell him—or trying to tell herself—but he understood most of it. He opened his wallet and showed her a photo. "My little boy," he said. "He died when he was only three years old." He wasn't being maudlin—there was no mawkishness in him; he was just showing her a picture of the way things were. "You're very fortunate if you think time passes quickly. For me it moves very slowly, giving me all the leisure I need to endure my sorrow." He smiled. "You can grow incredibly old when every hour seems to last forever."

And that was that.

She sat there a moment, smoking her cigarette and listening to the pianist play cadenzas. Then she picked up her mink, her purse, and the package containing the sweater. "Excuse me a second," she said.

She never came back. She spared him.

The Eye followed her. She walked along the pavement, her head bowed, her coat hanging on her shoulder. He moved behind her, almost at her side.

It was dusk. The street lamps were on; the hurrying streams of shoppers pushed around them. It was cold and wet and slippery, a Christmas-card evening, adorned with colored lights and wreaths, clamoring with bells and car horns, bright with golden shop windows shining on the snow. And she was just in front of him, only inches away, her cheeks glowing, her breath misty, her woolen *cagoule* sparkling with dots of frost. She pulled on her mink. He reached out, held it by the collar as she slipped her arms into the sleeves. She didn't notice. She was crying.

He sent his shepherding love ahead of her, parting the crowd so that she could pass untouched. At the intersections he changed the stoplights from green to red, blocking the traffic so that she could cross the streets in safety.

He would never forget this particular twilight. Years later, looking back across all their voyages together, this walk along Penn Boulevard would become his fondest memory. He would wake from a deep sleep in the dead of night and remember Philadelphia, Christmas, and the snow. He would hear the far-off carols playing their evensong and taste the winter air they breathed and feel the frozen grief of the solitude that divided them. *That was the year I gave her a pear*, he would tell the darkness.

"All flights have been canceled," the girl behind the counter said.

"For how long?"

"Just until the blizzard lets up some. You'll probably be able to leave tonight, if you don't mind waiting."

Joanna checked her luggage and sat down in the lounge. The airport was jammed with stranded passengers standing at the windows glaring up at the black sky. A charter mob, submerged in baggage, filled one corner of the room in a vast sprawl. A young man behind her was complaining shrilly to two Japanese, "Well, if I'm not in D.C. by noon tomorrow, maybe I ought to take a train."

She tried to read, then gave it up and just sat back and waited. Her finger was bothering her. She bit it gently, massaged it. A piped choir was singing "O Little Town of Bethlehem." Then an orchestra played Erich Wolfgang Korngold film scores. "I knew coming to Philly was a mistake," the young man behind her wailed. Frank Sinatra sang "Strangers in the Night." "It is to be wondered at," one of the Japanese said, "why snowplows do not unearth the runways."

Then the loudspeaker called her name, her real name.
She jumped up, astonished. She thought she'd dozed off
and simply dreamed it. The announcement was repeated.
She went over to the information desk. A hostess gave her
a small gift-wrapped package. "A gentleman left this for
you," she said.

"When?"

"Just a few minutes ago."

"Who? Who was it?"

"He didn't leave his name."

Joanna opened it. It contained a large fresh yellow pear
in a cellophane bag. Pinned to it was a card. She pulled it
off, read it. Printed on it was a handwritten greeting:
HAPPY BIRTHDAY!

She looked around the lounge, her eyes narrowing. She
saw the young man talking to the two Japanese. She saw a
Lufthansa steward. She saw a man in a parka, another
man bundled in furs like an Eskimo, two boys holding skis,
another boy carrying a guitar.

"Where are you, you sonofabitch?" she whispered.

She saw several charter flight men drinking cans of
beer, a man in an El Al uniform, a black reading *Oui*, a
man in a Chesterfield reading *Playgirl*, another man reading a paper, another smoking a pipe, another asleep . . .

She walked over to the man in the parka, squinted at
him. Then she moved to the black and scrutinized him
closely. He glanced up at her. "Anything I can do for you,
ma'am?" he asked uneasily. She walked on, passing the
Eye, and stood before the man in the Chesterfield. He
smiled at her politely. "I don't think we'll get out of here
tonight," he said. She went back to her chair and sat down.
She shrugged and ate the pear.

At ten o'clock the loudspeaker announced that there
would be no more takeoffs until tomorrow morning.
Joanna was asleep. A janitor woke her, rattling a mop and
bucket in her ear. "Hey!" he yelled. "We're closing up!"

"Merry Christmas," she said.

"Yeah," he growled.

She went outside. The young man who had to be in
Washington, D.C. by noon tomorrow was running around
trying to find a taxi. "I'm going to catch a train," he told
her.

"Me too."

"Where are you going?"

"Baltimore."

"I'm heading in that direction myself. Be my guest!"

His name was Henry Innis. He was an antiques dealer from Alexandria, thirty-one years old, unmarried, and at the time of his death was carrying approximately twenty-nine thousand dollars in his briefcase, the tax-free commission of a furniture auction he'd negotiated that afternoon in Philadelphia.

Killing him was no problem. At a quarter to twelve they went to Penn Station and caught a Washington local. There were almost no other passengers aboard. They had a bottle of bourbon, and he died of arsenic poisoning somewhere after Wilmington.

The Eye was in the coach behind theirs, doing a crossword puzzle. At the Aberdeen stop he glanced out the window and saw her crossing the platform, going into the waiting room. The train was already moving. He ran up the aisle and jumped out the door.

It was three o'clock in the morning. She walked through the cold bleak empty streets, muttering to herself. She found a church that was open and slept in a pew until dawn. The Eye spent the rest of the night sitting on a bench in a transept, reading a prayerbook. There were a dozen other derelicts there—bums, drunks, nighthawks lighting candles, old women with rosaries, one fat man in a Santa Claus outfit snoring behind the altar. A roving dip moved in on Joanna. She woke just as he was reaching for her purse. She drove him off, then went back to sleep. A teenage fag tried to pick up the Eye.

"Christmas head?" he whispered.

"Get lost."

The boy backed away into the shadows. The Eye looked up at the statues. St. Joseph, St. Anthony, St. Mary, St. Christopher . . . and one he didn't recognize. He went over to it and read the name on the plaque. *Saint Rita.* He'd never heard of her. She was in a pale blue gown trimmed with silver. A golden flower glowed on her throat. She had a Modigliani profile. He dropped a quarter into the slot and took a candle from the rack. He lit it, fixed it before her. *O dark saint,* he prayed. *Protect my two girls.*

*Don't let the sharks eat them. Keep the fucking FBI away.
And give Maggie shelter from the cold tonight.*

And tell me—what is a goddamned capital in Czechoslovakia?

At six o'clock they caught a Greyhound back to Philadelphia. By nine they were in the airport again. Joanna ate an enormous breakfast—scrambled eggs, wheatcakes, a filet mignon, a salad, pie. Then she checked out her luggage and flew to St. Louis.

They rented two cars and followed the Mississippi south through Waterloo, Red Bud, Chester, Carbondale, Ware, and Thebes. She spent the rest of the year in a motel in a place called Mound City near Cairo. Her name here was Victoria Chandler (blond wig).

On New Year's Eve she went to a bar in Wickliffe, a rat-eared clip joint filled with tough-looking drunks. The Eye's radar picked up the jinxed vibes and he tried to warn her out of the place.

Get up and leave, Joanna.
Just a couple of drinks.
You've already had five.
Get away from me! Who are you, anyway?
Go home to bed.
Who's talking to me?
Come on, let's split!
Leave me alone!

By two in the morning she was petrified. A jukebox was yowling country music. There were only a half-dozen hardcore boozers left at the bar. One of them, a big truckdriver type, closed in on her. He leaned across the table, took her by the shoulder, shook her. "Hey, blondie," he said. "Let's go outside and get some air." She flopped and wallowed in her chair, trying to rise. He grabbed her arms, yanked her to her feet. He dropped her, and she slid to the floor. The jackals at the bar watched and cackled.

The Eye came out of his corner. "Beat it," he told the trucker. "I'll take care of her."

The trucker pushed him away. "Buzz off, fuckhead! The broad's with me!" Luckily he was too drunk to hit anything. The Eye sidestepped the first two meat-cleaver blows and pounded him in the stomach. The truck driver went down, came up swinging murderously. The Eye caught a wild left across the cheek, jarring his teeth, then got behind him and clubbed him on the back of the neck, decking him again. This time he stayed down. Nobody else tried anything.

The Eye lifted Joanna, took her purse, pulled her to the door.

Outside he dragged her across the parking lot, found her keys in the purse, unlocked her car, heaved her awkwardly into the rear seat. He found her paperback *Hamlet* in the purse, too. He held it under the light and leafed through its pages. Hundreds of lines and passages were circled in red and Xed in orange and underlined in black and asterisked in green and blue and brown. He read a verse at random:

> . . . from her melodious lay
> To muddy death.

The drunks were stumbling out of the bar, howling and singing. He drove through the lot to the highway, honking his horn as he passed them.

"Happy New Year!" they shouted.

The rising sun woke her, burning through the windshield in a shower of pink lava. She sat up in the back seat, opened the door, peered around. The car was parked on the bank of the river. She climbed out to the ground, pulled off her wig, threw it aside. She leaned against the fender and held her head, moaning. Then she whirled, snatched up her purse from the front seat, searched it frantically. She found her money, counted it. It was all there. She sagged with relief, hanging on the door, her knees trembling. She sat down on the rocks, put her face in her hands. The tremors passed. She bit her left index, rubbed it against her knee. She looked at the sky, at the river. She kicked off her shoes, lifted her skirt, removed her stockings. She rose, undressed, hung her soiled clothing across the hood.

Nude, she waded into the icy water. She dived lithely into the swift current and swam in a wide semicircle away from the bank.

The Eye, standing in a copse up on the edge of the road, watched her, smiling ruefully.

He hoped she wasn't planning to drown herself, because he didn't know how to swim.

Fifteen

Joanna drove across western Kentucky to the Green River. In Rockport it was raining, and she skidded off the road into a fence. No real damage was done, but she was finally forced to do something about her myopia—contact lenses.

The Rockport Post Office provided the Eye with her federal *Wanted* poster; he hadn't realized just how hot she was. The composite ID portrait was an almost exact facsimile of her face. The nose strip was off, but the rest of her features were a perfect likeness. She was identified as Ella Dory AKA Mrs. Jerome Vight AKA Mary Linda Kane AKA Mrs. Rex Hollander AKA Ada Larkin. Ada Larkin! That really jolted him. It meant they'd traced her as far as Miami. How? The bastards, they'd probably checked the passenger lists of every flight out of Savannah the day Hollander's forty-grand check was cashed. He had to hand it to the motherfuckers—they were really efficient. Would they uncover her Roxane Devorak and Victoria Chandler identities now and follow her to Michigan and Philadelphia and St. Louis? No, he didn't see how they could do that. And yet . . .

In his hotel room that night he watched a TV movie about a convict, escaped from a chain gang, pursued by bloodhounds. He kept trudging through streams and swamps to throw the dogs off his scent, but then he had to cross a desert and the posse caught him. That was Joanna's problem, too. Her trail was too obvious, and she was running out of water to cover her tracks. Changing wigs and names just wasn't enough anymore.

She drove on toward Louisville—Dan "Ken Tuck" Kenny's former theater of operations. He tried to bring Kenny to mind but couldn't recall his face. Christ! How long ago had that been? Fresno, LA, the bookstore, Ralph Forbes, the clinic, Jessica, the cemetery on the banks of the San Joaquin River. . . . Had she killed Kenny? Yes . . . no . . . he'd died in the pen. They'd traveled down so many roads together, stopping at so many places! Now they were on Route 60, somewhere south of the Ohio River, passing through towns called Hawesville, Cloverport, Hardinsburg, Irvington. . . .

It was a bright, windy January afternoon. A girl stood on the edge of the highway, hitchhiking. She wore jeans, GI shoes, a pointed cap, and a combat jacket. She was blonde, freckled, no more than seventeen or eighteen. Her name— he learned much later—was Becky Yemassee.

Joanna picked her up.

Miles later they turned off the road into a narrow dirt track and disappeared into a woods. He stopped, afraid to follow them too closely. Where the hell were they going? Was there a village back there in the sticks? Or a farm? Or a house? He waited ten . . . fifteen . . . twenty minutes. He was just about to drive after them when the girl reappeared, running. An old Dodge Royal Lancer with a growling motor came speeding up the highway. A boy wearing a bowler with the brim cut off was driving it. He skidded over to the girl, opened the door. She jumped in beside him, and they zoomed away like Bonnie and Clyde.

The Eye drove into the track. He found Joanna's car parked in a clearing. All her luggage was open and her clothing strewn about the ground. She was lying in the front seat, unconscious, the cut on her forehead a neat, professional knockout blow, probably from a sap. He cleansed it with after-shave lotion. Then he searched her purse, the bags, and the car. He couldn't find any money. Bonnie Freckles must have taken it all.

She came out of the woods a half-hour later—on foot.

She was wearing slacks, boots, and a sweater, carrying an airline bag strapped to her shoulder. She walked toward Irvington. She looked like a farmboy striding to town to buy a sack of oats. She'd removed her wig, and the wind blew her hair across her face. The blow on the forehead didn't seem to bother her. Neither did the loss of her money. She was whistling . . . in fact, she was laughing. A mile past the track she stopped, picked up a rock, and dropped it into her bag.

Then she began hitchhiking.

A Honda sedan picked her up. The Eye followed it. It turned north and drove along the Ohio. It pulled into a junkyard beside the ruins of a jetty. He watched the driver take her in his arms, watched them kiss, watched her strike him across the skull with the stone. She took his wallet, dumped him into a ditch on his back, then drove back to 60.

She turned into the dirt track, left the sedan in the clearing, and drove her own car out to the highway.

During the next two weeks she repeated the performance twelve times, hitchhiking back and forth from Louisville to Huntington and from Danville to Bowling Green. One busy afternoon on Route 68, between Campbellsville and Edmondton, she hit four men in a row. Only two of her victims died.

In late February, while every state trooper in Kentucky was out looking for her, she slipped down to Nashville.

She was Nita Iqutos from Peru, with a wig of long black hair plaited in Indian braids. Her English had a warm cello accent. She was a reporter from some Lima or Quito or Santiago magazine, in town doing a series of articles on "the sound." She probably even had a press card, if anybody asked her for one. But nobody did.

Associating her with the hitchhiking bandit the Kentucky newspapers called "the Highway Harpy" was just unthinkable.

The Eye didn't know how much money she had accumulated, but she was still drinking cognac and smoking Gitanes. And she gambled every night. She moved in with a folksinger named Duke Foote. He was the coyote-voiced balladeer whose jukebox favorite "Texas Freeways" sold nine hundred thousand records. She hooked him as soon as they met because he was impotent and a fairly nice guy and, since he didn't snort coke or debase minors, the fuzz left him alone. Their photo appeared in the Grapevine section of *Playboy*, which made their relationship more or less official:

Interviewed during a recent recording session in Nashville, big Duke admitted shyly that he was thinking seriously about 'goin' to see the preacher man one o' these days 'stead o' always shackin' up like a dang sinner.' Fiery and fiercely Catholic Nita is just the gal to lead him back to the path of righteousness.

The Eye cringed and compared her photo to the ID composite he'd stolen from a post office. But there was really nothing to worry about. Nita Iqutos bore no resemblance at all to Ada Larkin or those other women.

In the spring Duke went to New York, leaving her alone in his mansion in Franklin. The Eye had been living in a motel out on Route 31, and now he visited her every night, like a lover, prowling through the gardens and looking through the windows, watching her cook supper and read and listen to records and, usually, get drunk alone. One evening she pretended she was blind and groped through the rooms for hours, tapping a cane and holding out a cup for alms. And one Saturday night a pack of Duke's turned-on friends showed up and staged an orgy. While they were carpeting the living room floor with their calisthenics, she sat by herself in another room listening to the "Emperor" Concerto. One of the girls crawled out of the bodies and joined her. She was blond, freckled, winsome; her nakedness wasn't yet altogether nubile, and she looked slightly lost. "Can I come in here with you?" she asked. "I'm not into this group sex bit."

It was Becky Yemassee.

Joanna locked the door and slapped her. Becky screeched. But everybody was screeching. Her cry of terror sounded like just another orgasm.

"What did you do with my goddamned money, you fucking brat!"

"Moby took it!"

"Who's Moby?"

"My guy. He said he had to go up t' Terre Haute and he cut out and left me in Shelbyville and he took all the bread with him 'cept two hundred dollars he give me and that was the last time I ever seen him!"

"What's your name?"

"Becky Yemassee. And you're Nita, Duke's chick?"

"Yes."

"I didn't recognize you. What's with your hair, like?"

"It's a wig."

"Yeah? Can I try it on?"

Joanna pulled off the wig and handed it to her. Becky put it on her head, walked over to a mirror. She looked like an Aztec sacrifice. "I'm goin' to get me one," she chattered. "Wearin' this hustlin' my ass, I can charge the motherfuckers a hundred bucks a throw."

"Hustling your ass? Is that what you're doing?"

"No way, I'm goin' to be a singer. As soon as I can find a good secondhand gittar not too expensive. I only hustle when I gotta."

"Sing something for me."

And Becky sang "I Heard the Crash on the Highway but I Didn't Hear Nobody Pray."

Joanna's verdict was merciful. "Nifty peachy," she said dryly.

"Kind of jagged," Becky admitted. "But that can be fixed when it's recorded. Listen to that!" In the other room the crowd was making zoo noises. "That's the *real* Nashville sound!"

"Come and take a shower," Joanna said. "You smell like an alligator."

It began to rain.

Later the Eye climbed up the veranda lattice to the bedroom window. They were sitting on the bed, nude. Joanna was holding Becky on her knees, hugging her to her breast, rocking her gently. They were both sobbing. He watched them and thought, *By what way is the light parted? Hath the rain a father? Out of whose womb came the ice?* He wondered where the hell he'd heard that before.

Becky was from Charleston, South Carolina. Her real name was Azalea Goche. "My ma come from Orangeburg," she explained. "That's how I got that shitty

name Azalea, from the Edisto Gardens there, full o' aza-
leas. And Goche, shit! How do you like that! Azalea
Goche! I changed it when I took off. Did you ever read
Rebecca by Daphne du Maurier? I read it twice. Did you
ever see the movie on TV with Joan Fontaine? She's probably one of the most beautiful things on earth! I was almost
goin' to call myself Rebecca Fontaine, but it sounded too
phony. I picked Yemassee instead. It's a little town down
near the Georgia borderline. It makes me keep remem-
berin' where I'm from."

Her mother had worked all her life in whorehouses in
Walterboro, Charleston, and Folly Beach. "That's where I
grew up. In bordellos. By the time I was ten I knew fifty
different ways to give hand jobs. I used to jerk off marines
for a quarter. 'You watch it,' Ma used to say. 'One of 'em
may be your daddy.' That was her idea of witty repartee."

Her mother died when she was eleven. "A couple o' shit-
heads from Parris Island took her swimmin' one Sunday.
She was bombed and as soon as the waves hit her she
dropped dead." Becky ran away to Columbia, then to
Charlotte, then to Knoxville. "I jerked off guys all the way
across three fuckin' states. In railroad stations, in johns, in
airports, in parkin' lots, in Greyhounds, in drive-ins, in
movies, once in the back of a hook-and-ladder with a fire-
man. In Charlotte I raised my price to a buck and a half.
But I never went down on them, because I can't take that
stink. Puttin' it in my mouth would be like eatin' moldy
baloney. I couldn't do it even with Moby. He smelled par-
ticularly foul down there."

She met Moby in Knoxville, and he took her to Indianapolis. "He was a baseball player. A shortstop for the Yan-
kees, but they bounced him for snortin' coke. He was also
on sugar and copolots and Emma and you name it. He was
like zonked out forever in perpetual Happy Landingville.
He thought up the hitchhiking gimmick with a blackjack.
We tried it out a couple of times in Indiana, then came
down to Kentucky where I met you and hit the big loot.
When you picked me up that afternoon near Irvington I
said to myself, 'Jesus H. Christ! She's prettier than Joan
Fontaine!' I didn't belt you too hard—I hope you appreciate that. I didn't want to leave a scar on your forehead.

Afterwards I told Moby, the prick, 'Shit! I hope she forgives me.' You do forgive me, don't you, Nita?"

"Sure, Becky."

"I adore your accent! It gives me goose pimples! I never met anybody who had so many different ways of talkin'. And so many different ways of bein' different. You keep changin' all the time."

"The devil hath the power to assume a pleasing shape."

They lived together for three months while Duke Foote was in New York. The Eye would hang on the lattice by the window all night, listening to them talk and laugh and weep and make love and read to each other. They read *Rebecca* and *Gone with the Wind* and *Hamlet* and *Variety*. They visited the Shiloh battlefield and Lookout Mountain and the Atomic Museum in Oak Ridge. In May they went to the Cotton Carnival in Memphis. Joanna taught her to drive. She bought her clothes and had her hair fixed. Gradually Becky turned into a pleasing shape herself. She became sleek and groomed, chic and perfumed. She grew up. And one morning when the Eye saw the two of them walking side by side in Centennial Park, he could hardly tell them apart.

When Duke came back to Franklin, he kicked them out of the house. They moved into an apartment in Nashville, but Joanna was running out of money. They bought two pistols with silencers from a shady gunsmith, and one Saturday night, masked and wearing men's suits, they stuck up a gas station in Lebanon. The take netted them enough to pack their bags and fly to San Francisco.

The money from the sale of Cora Earl's jewels was still in the safe-deposit box in Oakland. While Joanna went into the bank to collect it, Becky waited outside. So did the Eye, sweating with panic. He examined every foot of the street but couldn't spot any stakeouts—which, of course, didn't mean a thing. Maybe the Feds were inside. Or miraculously, maybe they just didn't know about the box.

A half-hour passed. He was convinced they had her. He almost vomited with terror. He saw tomorrow's headlines in the sky: HUSBAND SLAYER CAUGHT! SPIDER WIDOW ARRESTED! FBI TRAPS MULTIMURDER-

ESS! NATIONWIDE HUNT FOR DEATH-BRIDE ENDS
IN OAKLAND CAPTURE!

Then she appeared, striding nonchalantly along the
pavement, whistling, carrying a sackful of dollars.

At lunch in the airport dining room he listened to them
trying to make plans.

"Where do you want to go, Becky?"

"How about Miami?"

"No, not Miami."

"Why not?"

"I have to keep away from Florida."

"What about Hawaii then?"

"That's no good either."

"Then LA. I never been there."

"I'd rather avoid LA too."

"Shit! Have you got anything against New York?"

"As a matter of fact, yes."

"Fuck!"

They spent three months at Lake Tahoe and six months
in New Orleans. Then, in an Opel Manta, they drove
through Texas, Colorado, Wyoming, Montana, and north-
ern Idaho to Washington. They stayed in Seattle for two
months.

"In the whorehouse in Walterboro," Becky said, "there
was this one room filled with toys. Dolls and teddy bears
and blocks and little cars and whatnot. Sometimes Ma
would lock me in there all day long." The two girls were at
a topless beach near Townsend on Puget Sound, lying in
the sand, eating pears and sunbathing. Joanna was reading
Beethoven by Romain Rolland.

"But first she'd make me take off my clothes. I'd be in
there bare-assed, dig. I must've been about eight or nine. I
didn't like it. That fuckin' room scared me. There was
something spooky about it. I'd start cryin' and she'd come
in and slap me around and say, 'Play with your goddamned
toys, you little cunt!' Well, there was holes in the wall, see.
I found out later there was always a couple of guys in the
next room, watchin' me. I was part of the floor show. How
do you like that?"

"Didn't anything pleasant ever happen to you?" Joanna
asked.

"Just you." Becky smiled wistfully. "Everything else that happened to me was shitty. But the point is—" She glanced around them, scowling. "The point is there's holes in the wall here too. Somebody's watchin' us."

"No there isn't."

"Oh yeah there is. In New Orleans too. And all while we was drivin' up here. And back in Nashville too. Somebody's watchin' us."

"I used to think that all the time. But it's just an effect."

"A what? What is it?"

"A fancy." She closed her book and lit a Gitane. "We create things, you see. Out of the air and the wind and the people around us and impressions and sensations and all that. And out of ourselves also, our thoughts and our fears and our guilts. And our prayers. And these things take form and come around us and stare at us and even talk to us sometimes. Listen—" And she looked at the crowd and whispered, "Are you still there, old buddy?" She laughed and sat up. "Did you hear that? He answered me!"

"What did he say?"

"He said, 'Yes, I'm here!' "

"What're you, flippin' or what?"

"Not in the least!" She put her arm around her. "I hope he'll always be there. He's comforting. Let us come before his presence with thanksgiving."

"Shit."

They went to Reno and Vegas and lost all their money playing roulette. They sold the Opel and flew across the country to Portland, Maine. Joanna had another cache here, dating from the years before the Eye knew her—four thousand dollars in a safe-deposit box in a bank in Westbrook, rented under the name of Miss Faye Jacobs (dark wig). And two thousand more farther north in another bank in Auburn, where she was known as Mrs. Paula Jason (no wig).

They spent the next ten months driving west in an old Peugeot 604, taking their time, spending three or four or five weeks at every stopover: Syracuse, Toledo, Indianapolis, Des Moines, Omaha, Denver, Salt Lake City (eight weeks!), Carson City.

By the time they got to California they were broke again.

Operating out of Pasadena, they unpacked their pistols and silencers, put on their masks and men's suits and stuck up a grocery store in Sierra Madre and a haberdashery in Azusa. And a Hugo shoestore (*Founded in 1867*) in Alta Loma.

It was eight o'clock, closing time. The last customer left, a rancher carrying a new pair of boots. The boy behind the counter was alone. He was in his twenties, spare and long-haired and not very good-looking. His name was Finch. He probably hated his job, hated his boss and the store and Alta Loma and the smell of leather and feet and socks—or so the Eye assumed, reading about the stickup in the papers the next day. Actually, though, there was no way of knowing what Finch thought about anything, if he thought at all. But he couldn't have been very bright. Sacrificing his life for a cash box filled with someone else's money was extremely noble and conscientious and proved an unmistakable dedication to his employer's interests, but it was an asinine thing to do. Perhaps, if he had survived, he would have been given a raise. This could have motivated his action. Or perhaps he was in love with the manager's daughter and hoped to win her hand in marriage as a reward for his heroism. Or then again, perhaps he was just exactly what he appeared to be, a dumb and earnest thrall with a shoe horn hanging from a string around his neck.

As the two girls came through the door aiming their guns at him, he reached under the counter, opened a drawer, and lifted out a 357 Magnum.

"Shit and corruption!" Becky shouted.

He shot her in the stomach just as she pulled the trigger and blew away all his vocal cords.

Joanna emptied the cash box into her purse and carried Becky out to the Peugeot. She drove toward San Bernardino at seventy miles per hour.

She left her, bleeding and gibbering, on the doorstep of a hospital in Rialto, then checked into a motel near Riverside. So did the Eye.

Becky's death was announced on the eleven o'clock news. She was identified from her driver's license. The newscaster looked appropriately grim when he mentioned her age. She was seventeen years old.

The Eye heard someone knock softly on the door of the unit next to his. "Yes?" a man's voice called. "Who's there?"

"Can I come in for a minute, please?" Joanna answered.

The Eye looked out the window. She was standing before the cabin, one hand behind her back. The door opened, the man grinned at her. "Why, sure thing!" he said. "Come on in!"

The Eye heard the ebullient *poooooff!* of the silencer as she shot him in the face. The body fell back into the room with a crash. She walked to the adjacent cabin and knocked on the door. "What's up?" another man shouted. "Please let me in," she said.

She killed seven men that night.

Sixteen

Five long years passed; five Christmases and five birthdays. And nine more men . . . no, ten, eleven . . . the Eye tried to remember.

Ten or eleven.

She married three of them. One husband was a doctor. (Just like—what was his name? Years and years ago, right after she'd killed Paul Hugo. Brice! Dr. James Brice! His bones were still buried under the thickets outside The Birdcage.) Doctor Number Two was smothered under a pillow while sleeping off the effects of his wedding champagne. After Joanna left, the Eye searched the room and found a dozen credit cards in a valise. He kept them, and for the next year they paid for all his gas and cars and meals and plane tickets. He even bought a new suit (his fourth) with one of them.

He found this to be an ideal means of economizing. So once or twice a year, on moonless nights, he would unload his .45, and on a lonely street or in a parking lot outside a bar or restaurant he would waylay someone, hold him up, and relieve him of all his cards. Thus he was always plentifully supplied with credit.

His gambling enhanced his budget, too. One New Year's Eve, at a roulette wheel in Reno, he played the zero and it bounced up. He won all the chips on the table plus thirty-five times his own *mise*. This solved his financial problems for the next two years.

Joanna wasn't quite as lucky. She lost almost continuously. In a casino in Tulsa she dropped the entire take from one of her marriages in a single night. And she was drinking much too much. She was still nimble and lovely, but she had to spend more and more time in gymnasiums and swimming pools and beauty parlors to keep herself presentable.

The names Nita Iqutos, Faye Jacobs, and Paula Jason were added to the AKA list on her poster in the post offices. Because of her association with Becky, the Feds docketed her with the Finch shooting in Alta Loma and the motel cataclysm in Riverside. She was now one of the five Most Wanted Women in the United States.

They came after her slowly and massively, like a moving glacier. But they couldn't overtake her. Although she blazed a trail, she never stopped fleeing. And because she had no direction, they were unable to intercept her.

She came to Houston, and Houston, like LA, turned a page in her life.

This was Duke Foote country, celebrated in his still famous song "Texas Freeways":

> *On Route 59*
> *I pine an' I pray*
> *Come rain or come shine*
> *Goin' to find her some day*

Lovelady! Are you on Route 45
Lovelady! Are you dead or alive?
Lovelady! Are you in Galveston Bay?*

She met Chuck Estes, the son of oilman Bertie Estes, who had been one of President Johnson's cronies. Chuck was forty, with a low forehead, a demented teenager's mentality, and several million dollars. He wore tailor-made buckskin shirts, dude cowboy suits, a five-gallon hat, and spurs. His friends called him "Chuck Wagon."

He picked her up at a barbecue in Liberty. He drove her back to Houston in his zebra-striped Thunderbird and they had drinks at the Longhorn Grill.

"So you're from LA, huh?" His conversation was as flat and barren as a prairie. "That's a jumpin' burg all right. We got an office there now. Whole floor of a buildin' on Sunset Boulevard. I was there last month. Flew into San Diego and I said, 'Well what the devil, might as well go on up to LA and see some action.' Stayed there two and a half weeks. Stayed at the Beverly Wilshire Hotel. I saw some action all right. The walls kept shakin'. 'What's that?' I asked a feller in the elevator. 'Earthquake,' he said. 'The whole city's going to crack open like a watermelon one of these days.' And bango! Down in the lobby a great big hunk of the ceiling dropped on the floor! I said to myself, 'Hey!' I hopped in a taxicab and drove over to the office fast. Everything was shipshape there though, except—hey, waiter! Couple of more here, please!—Except all the windows was busted out. Cost us fifteen hundred dollars to put in new panes. LA—no thank you. New York's my town. Now that's an A-A-A place, Anything, anytime, anywhere! 'New York and Los Angeles,' my dad used to say. 'Two bookends for a vacuum.' What's this you're smokin'? Grass? Gee-tans. Let me try one." Then his attention roved to the other side of the room to a girl in a backless dress sitting at the bar. "Excuse me," he said. And he walked over to her.

And that's how it happened—casually and cruelly. They began laughing together. He bought her a drink.

Joanna waited for him to come back to the table. He

* *Texas Freeways.* Words and music by Duke Foote. © Lone Star Publishers, Inc.

didn't. She sat there for three quarters of an hour. He never even glanced at her. He simply forgot she was there. She was white-lipped with anger. She ordered another cognac. Couples sitting at the other tables watched her, smiling.

The Eye watched, too, hoping she wouldn't get drunk and cause a commotion. She didn't. She just left.

And the page turned.

> *Lovelady on the highway*
> *Lovelady on the byway*
> *Lovelady ain't you ever comin' my way*
> *Down them long long empty roads.*

She drove through Louisiana, Mississippi, Alabama, Georgia, and North Carolina, dropping a couple of grand at each stop in gambling clubs and backroom poker tables and, once in a while, at a racetrack. How much money did she have left? The Eye wasn't sure. How much of anything did she have left? How much spirit and stamina? How much endurance? He watched, appalled, as the chasm opened before her.

Her car broke down in Burnsville, N.C., and it cost four hundred dollars to have it repaired. She stayed in the town of Linville trying her old hitchhiking caper on the Blue Ridge Parkway; it just wouldn't work. On the first day she stood on the edge of the highway for three hours. Hundreds of cars passed. None stopped for her. She had lunch in a truckers' café, then went back to the road in the afternoon and stayed there until nine o'clock, waving her thumb like an automaton.

On the second day it rained. A gorilla in an Alfa picked her up, drove her into a field near Deep Gap, and tried to rape her. She got away from him with only a black eye and a lost contact lens and walked in the pounding thunderstorm all the way to Blowing Rock, where her car was parked. She spent a week in bed with a fever, reading *Look Homeward, Angel* by Thomas Wolfe.

When she left North Carolina she was wearing glasses. She drove to Virginia, sold her car in Portsmouth, tried to cash a bogus check in a bank in Virginia Beach but at the last minute panicked and fled. In May her landlady evicted her from her rooming house in Norfolk, impounding her luggage.

In Newport News she began shoplifting, stealing soap and toothpaste and canned soup and pears from supermarkets. She got caught only once—trying to lift a bottle of scotch. The clerk let her go—he even let her keep the bottle. She was in a drunken stupor for days afterwards, sleeping in parked cars and cabanas on the beach. A Pan Am stewardess on vacation picked her up in Hampton, and the two of them lived together for three weeks in a trailer camp. When the stewardess went back to work, Joanna floated up to Yorktown, where she lived in an abandoned shack in the dunes, keeping herself clean by bathing in the sea. She stole a dress from a clothesline and a pair of jeans from a sailboat anchored in the bay.

In Williamsburg the police never bothered her, the midsummer peninsula was swarming with drifters. She moved into an old boathouse on the James River. The Eye didn't know what to do for her. He bought a carton of groceries and left them on the wharf one night, but two kids passing in a canoe swiped everything. On another night he dropped a whole pile of credit cards in the boathouse mailbox, but Joanna never opened it.

Then her behavior turned weird, and she began roaming through the streets for hours and hours every day, going nowhere, just wandering around, up one block and down the other, stooped over, peering into gutters and bushes. These endless walks frightened him. She looked like a scurrying madwoman! He couldn't grasp what she was up to.

One afternoon she found a quarter on the sidewalk, and he finally understood.

She was looking for money!

On her next excursion he managed to drop a hundred-dollar bill on the pavement in front of her. When she saw it, she just couldn't believe it. She stood transfixed for an instant, then snatched it up and ran off with it, escaping like a bank robber into the other end of town.

Instead of spending it all on booze, as he thought she would, she had her hair cut and bought a new skirt, a blouse, and a pair of shoes.

She went to Richmond and got a job—in fact, several jobs, working in a grocery store for a while, then in a dry-cleaning place, then in a five-and-ten, then car-hopping in a drive-in, and finally as a chambermaid in the Eye's hotel.

She lived in a cheap room in a back street boarding-house, going to movies or to the public library on her days off. She read *The Good Earth* by Pearl Buck, *Death Comes for the Archbishop* by Willa Cather, *Barren Ground* by Ellen Glasgow, and *The Heart Is a Lonely Hunter* by Carson McCullers. Occasionally she'd go to a pool, but swimming seemed to exhaust her these days. She stopped drinking, then began again, then stopped again.

She grew old.

So did the Eye. He wore glasses now, and was plagued with rheumatism, sciatica, and a hernia. While she was working at the hotel, he spent all his days sitting in a comfortable armchair down in the lobby, doing crossword puzzles and gossiping with the house dick and bellhops. They thought he was a retired dentist from up north somewhere, in Richmond visiting his grandchildren. He was using his own name and credit card, so he had no reason to hide in corners. He enjoyed the repose. He always knew where she was, he had nothing to do but wait for her. She was going through one of her drying-out periods, and he knew she was saving her money, so there was no reason—for the moment, at least—to expect the worst.

One morning he overheard two swashbuckling traveling salesmen discussing her over their breakfast coffee.

"What do you think of that maid up on the tenth floor? That haircut of hers rouses me."

"She looks like a garbage man in drag."

"She'd be okay if she fixed herself up some, got good legs and a fine body."

"What're you talking about!"

"You take a close look at her the next time you see her. That's rainy afternoon ass, boy. She came into my room yesterday just when I was climbing out of the bathtub and I let her get a good look at Moe the Mole. She didn't mind."

"What'd she do?"

"Nothing. But, you know, if a determined fellow sort of grabbed her and put her down on the bed and pulled off her panties . . ."

"Hoo-hoooo!"

"She probably wouldn't say nothing, eh? Probably too afraid of losing her job to make a noise about it."

"Probably even go for it."

"Right on. Want to give it a try?"

"Both of us?"

"Sure. Round robin."

"Hoo-hoooo!"

The Eye went out and bought two sachets of horse from a pusher who operated around the Edgar Allan Poe shrine. He picked the lock of one of the salesmen's rooms and hid the stuff in a shoe in the closet. Later he had a chat with his friend the house dick.

"Say, you know those two drummers who are always cutting up in the bar?"

"Yeah, they're a pain in the ass. Elderly juvenile delinquents."

"What are they selling anyway?"

"I dunno. Plastics or something."

"They're not in the munitions business?"

"The munitions business! What makes you think that?"

"Well, I was eavesdropping on them in the coffee shop this morning—they didn't know I was listening—and I wasn't, actually, I just couldn't help hearing what they said . . ."

"Yeah?"

"They were talking about dynamite and TNT, and one of them said it was too dangerous to keep all the powder in here in the hotel. God, I thought maybe they had bombs or something in their rooms."

"Yeah? Dynamite? TNT?"

"That's what I thought they said. I probably misunderstood."

"Are you sure it wasn't STP? Or DMT?"

"Could be."

That evening the two salesmen were busted for possession of drugs.

* * *

A few days later, the house dick came up to him in the lobby, quivering with excitement. "See that guy that just left?"

The Eye was using a new aspirin, and his aches and pains bothered him only when he moved. He'd been sitting at the window, watching the rain and dozing blissfully, dreaming of the corridor. He woke, annoyed. "No. What guy?"

"A Federal."

"A which?"

"FBI. Checkin' on everybody stayin' at the hotel."

The Eye yawned. "Who's he looking for?"

"Murder suspect." The dick showed him the ID composite of Joanna. "They call this a composite portrait. It's made of strips, see—hair, eyes, nose, mouth, and chin."

"'Murder most foul, strange and unnatural.'"

"Beg pardon?"

"Is she at the hotel?"

"Nope. But if she's in Richmond, they'll get her sure as shit. You can't stay hid long from them guys."

That afternoon the Eye visited Joanna's boardinghouse, a musty, ancient brick building on the river bank. (During the siege of Petersburg Robert E. Lee's headquarters had been just down the street. All the cars parked along the curb had Confederate flags on their bumpers.) The poodle-faced little woman who ran the place received him in a damp parlor filled with bronze horses under glass domes.

"Federal Bureau of Investigation." He showed her a badge. "We're trying to locate a woman named Miss Nita Iqutos. Is she one of your tenants, ma'am?"

"No, sir," she barked at him. "There are no fugitives from justice residing in this house."

"Is there anyone here from Los Angeles?"

She looked startled. "Why, yes—Miss Vincent is from Los Angeles." (Joanna had been using her old LA alias—she had a social security number in that name.)

"Can I speak to Miss Vincent, please, ma'am?"

"She's at work."

"When will she be home?"

"Seven thirty."

"Would you tell her I'll be back at—" He glanced at his watch. "No, I can't make it this evening. Tell her I'll see

her tomorrow night around eight o'clock. Thank you,
ma'am."

He checked out of the hotel, said good-bye to the house
dick, tipped the bellhops, and took a cab back to the boardinghouse at seven thirty-five. Joanna came out the front
door at eight ten, carrying only her purse. But she was
bulky and moved with padded awkwardness, which meant
that she was wearing all her clothes under her raincoat.

He followed her to the railroad station. She bought a
ticket to Washington.

> *Amblin', strayin'*
> *Ramblin', prayin'*
> *I walk in the April sun*
> *Highwayin', laughin' an' cryin'*
> *Bywayin', livin' an' dyin'*
> *It's spring again on Route 61.*

She stayed in Washington for two months, living on her
savings, changing her name, wearing a new wig, emerging
from her crust of slatternliness, blossoming again. And she
met Yale Cyril Polk at a YMCA barn dance. He was sixty-
two, a retired National Gallery curator, a hearty, scholarly
bachelor, the author of a book called *From King Tut to the
Men's Room, a Study of Mural Erotica* (Stuyvesant Press,
$12.50).

He took her to Kennedy Center to see *Aïda*, *Der Flie-
gende Holländer*, and the New York City Ballet's production of *'Tis a Pity She's a Whore*. They went to movies and
Chinese restaurants, to a folk song festival, a table tennis
tournament, a baseball game, and an all-female wrestling
match. They spent a weekend together (but in separate
rooms) in Ocean City.

A woman followed them there.

The Eye who had grown not only rheumatic but also
careless during these last few years, almost missed her.
When he finally spotted her, he hobbled to cover, cursing
himself.

She sat in her car outside the motor court for two nights.
When Joanna and Yale Cyril Polk went strolling on the
boardwalk, she spied on them from the dunes. When they
danced and dined and played liars' dice in a bar, she

watched them through the windows. When they drove back to Washington, she was a half mile behind them all the way.

She was in her fifties, handsome, pert, and furious. It was her anger that convinced the Eye she couldn't possibly be a Bureau agent. She was too high-strung for that. He trailed her to an apartment house in Laurel. Her name was (Mrs.) Maybelle Danzig. She was a math teacher in a prep school in Rockville. Until just a few weeks ago she had been Yale Cyril Polk's steady girl friend. The D.C. wags called them Ma and Pa.

The Eye's radar, after a long sleep, was panting like a tea kettle, picking up storm warnings everywhere. He pilfered one of her love letters from Yale Cyril's mailbox.

Poor pathetic Lothario,

Be assured of one thing, you are mine, all
mine, and I mean that, you know Yale I do
not joke about such things with levity and
I will not let this vulgar little slut come
between us. I know you have a "roving eye"
and that has always amused me but this latest
escapade is just too outrageous for words
and I will not tolerate it. Be assured of
one thing I am not the kind of woman one just
"ditches" no sir! My late husband, God rest
his soul, is probably "turning over in his grave"
at the spectacle of my humiliation. But you
may be assured of one thing, your heartlessness
will not go unpunished Yale & there will be a
reckoning!
          Maybelle

On a warm afternoon in May Yale Cyril withdrew eight thousand dollars from his bank account. He picked up Joanna on K Street and they drove along the Potomac to Harpers Ferry where a justice of the peace married them. They had dinner in Frederick. They were to spend their honeymoon night in a motel near Westminster, then drive to Philadelphia and New York.

However, there was a change of plans.

Maybelle Danzig was waiting for them at the motel. It was time for the reckoning. She had a Lüger.

"I love you!" she screamed. And she shot Yale Cyril once in the leg and once in the back of the shoulder. She shot a hole in Joanna's valise. A man coming out of one of the units to see what all the noise was about was hit in the hip by a stray bullet. Another bullet killed a barking police dog. "I love you, I love you!" she shrieked again and again, and tried to fire a shot into her temple, but the gun jammed.

Joanna managed to escape in Yale Cyril's car. She drove to Baltimore, abandoned the car, threw her wig away, and walked to the Greyhound terminal.

She sat for hours in the waiting room, just staring at the floor.

Rain began splashing on the windows. She opened her valise, took out a raincoat, pulled it on over her wedding dress.

Then she bought a ticket for Trenton, N.J.

Seventeen

It was three o'clock in the morning when she climbed out of the bus. She put her valise in a locker and walked through the empty streets to State and Broad. She stood on the corner, looking up and down.

The Eye stepped into a doorway a half-block behind her. *What are you going to do now, Joanna?*

She walked up East State past the Bell Telephone Building and the post office, turned down Clinton to the railroad station. There was an all-night restaurant here, so she ate a sandwich and drank a cup of coffee.

I'm going home.

She walked to Tyler Street.

All the houses were gone. The whole block was a vast crater filled with high cranes reaching out of the darkness like dinosaurs' necks. A spotlight lit up a sign reading BATTLE MONUMENT PARK 4000 Apartments 20,000 Trees.

Shit! Then she laughed. *In my father's house are many homes!*

She went back to the terminal for her valise. In the morning she moved into a rooming house on Yard Avenue. In the afternoon she looked for a job. She was hired as a waitress in The Hessian Barracks on West State Street.

The Eye sat down at his usual place near the front windows. He opened a menu.

> TRY OUR SPECIAL 13
> ORIGINAL COLONIES BREAKFAST

> TRY OUR MARQUIS DE LAFAYETTE
> SALAD

He'd tried both. They sucked.

There were eight waitresses, two in each quarter of the restaurant, wearing Hessian grenadier tunics, tiny tricorn hats pinned atop periwigs, hip boots, and miniskirts. The half dozen or so tables in this corner of the room were Joanna's sector.

> TRY OUR BATTLE OF TRENTON
> ROAST BEEF

> TRY OUR DELAWARE CROSSING
> BAKE SHOP CORN BREAD &
> SODA BISCUITS

She came out of the kitchen, served a couple sitting in front of him.

"Hey, girlie!" someone called. "What about our coffee?"

"Yes, sir." She dropped a spoon. She was wearing her glasses. Her peruke was lopsided, her tricorn had come unpinned. She looked like a cartoon Betsy Ross.

> TRY OUR 1776 APPLE
> PANCAKES
>
> TRY OUR SPECIAL MERCER
> COUNTY BIVOUAC BRUNCH

"Miss! Miss!" a woman chirped, "can I have another napkin, please?"

"Yes, ma'am."

> TRY OUR $1.50 DAWN'S EARLY
> LIGHT EYE OPENERS

She dropped a knife.

"Honey!" a man shouted. "I don't want to rush you or anything like that, but we've been waiting here for almost fifteen minutes now."

"Yes, sir."

She finally came over to the Eye's table. "Good morning."

"Morning." He fumbled with the menu. "I'll have the—the—uhh—eggs with sausage and herbs." He had the shakes again. This was his *n*th meal in the place, but he always began quaking whenever she stood next to him. His trembling subsided in time, as it always did, thank God.

It was June. The window was open. The sun warmed the backs of his hands. Christ! She'd been working here in this ye fucking olde mess hall for two weeks—no, longer—eighteen days!

What are you doing, Joanna?

Waiting. She dropped an armful of menus.

Waiting for what?

Waiting. Waiting. She picked up the menus. *Waiting . . .*

The hostess hurried over to the Eye's table. She was plump and fussy and motherly and always in a state of crisis. "We're so crowded," she complained. "Would you mind very much sharing your table?"

"Help yourself," the Eye said.

"Thank you so much." She turned and called, "Over here, Lieutenant!"

Two men came across the room and sat down beside him. They were lean and cool and short haired. They wore shabby suits. One of them needed a shave. "Thanks," the lieutenant grinned. The Eye nodded politely. They picked up menus and ignored him.

Fuzz!

He closed down his radar, locked it. If he started sending out signals, he knew they would feel the vibes. They were pros, oldtimers, just as attuned to the beams as he was. He turned off all his switches, dials, and buttons.

"What was the sergeant so worked up about?" Shaggy Cheeks asked.

"Those junkies he grabbed on State Street," the lieutenant muttered. "One of them was only eleven years old."

"My God."

"Father's a teacher at Junior Three."

"You eat in this place often?"

"Once in a while. Since they closed Louie's joint there's not much choice."

The Eye glanced out the window. He had to say something. If he didn't, they'd notice. An innocent bystander wouldn't just sit here and clam up. He would have to try to start a conversation and let them brush him off.

"Beautiful day," he remarked. They smiled at him tiredly. "Trenton's a lovely city. You fellows live here?"

"Yes."

"I'm just passing through myself. My son's at Princeton. Going to drive up and see him and—"

Joanna came to the table, and they ordered. The Eye asked for a pear. She walked off, colliding with another waitress.

"Watch it!" the girl yelped.

"Sorry," Joanna gasped. She fled to the kitchen.

The lieutenant watched her, chuckling sardonically. "Very attractive chick," he drawled.

"Gorgeous," the other sneered. "That monkey suit! It's too much!"

They bolted down their food and left. The Eye ate his pear and drank two cups of coffee. When she came to gather up the dishes he whispered to her, "Policemen always make me nervous."

She looked at him. "What?"

"Those two—they were cops."

She shrugged indifferently.

Balls! She just wasn't reacting. He sat back and stared at the menu.

>TRY OUR INDEPENDENCE DAY
>PORT WINE MELON & CLOVER
>HONEY BAKED GRAPEFRUIT

He had to get her out of here. How?

>TRY OUR HESSIAN SOLDIER
>STRUDEL

Fuck all! How?

>TRY OUR YANKEE DOODLE
>FRENCH FISH COURSES

>*Filets de sole aux raisins à la*
>*Thomas Jefferson*
>*Médaillons de colin à la*
>*Ben Franklin*
>*Brochet grillé à la John*
>*Hancock*

There was only one way.

He took a train to Camden and bought a car—a Stone Age Porsche with a rattling washing-machine motor. He paid for it in cash, not bothering to use one of his fake BankAmericards. This proved to be a lucky inspiration, saving him from a rap later, when the police investigated the car's ownership.

He drove it back to Trenton and moved into a motel on the Washington Crossing turnpike.

He then rented another car, a Chevette, which he drove to the motel, too.

He bought six blank cartridges in a sporting goods store on Greenwood Avenue, and loaded them into the clip of his .45.

He went to the Broad Street National Bank and cashed ten one-hundred-dollar traveler's checks. He bundled the money into a package of twenty fifties and put it into an attaché case.

Then he went back to The Hessian Barracks for supper.

Joanna was passing and repassing, carrying trays and menus. He waved to her but she didn't see him.

He opened the case, took out the wad of money, pretended to conceal it as he counted it. He recounted it. Then he counted it again. And again.

Finally she walked over to him, removing her glasses and pinching her nose. "What will it be tonight?" she asked listlessly.

"I don't care." He held the wad in both hands, like an offering. "Anything at all. I—" He was trembling. He looked up at her. She was staring out the window. He saw her throat rising out of the open collar of the tunic. He saw the powdery curve of her cheek. He saw her green eyes shining over him, past him, beyond him. He looked down and saw her hand on the table, the crooked finger just beside him.

She put on her glasses and blinked at him. "I beg your pardon . . ."

"How about an omelet." He dropped the bills back into the attaché case. "And a salad or something."

"Sure." He set the case on an empty chair. "Fine."

She walked off. She stopped, looked over her shoulder at the chair.

Whew.

By eight o'clock half the tables were filled. The lieutenant came in, alone. He sat down on the opposite side of the room.

She brought the Eye his omelet.

"He's back again," he said.

"Who is?"

"That policeman."

"Do you want to order your dessert now?"

Waiting, she whispered. *Waiting . . .*

The kitchen door swung open, knocking a carafe out of her hand. It smashed to the floor.

A loudmouth shouted, "Hit him again!"

She brought him his salad. He tried to speak to her. He couldn't.

All the tables were filled. A line was forming behind the entranceway rope.

She brought him another salad, covering the table with a jungle of lettuce. "Two for the price of one?" he quipped.

"What?" She stared blankly at the two huge bowls. "Oh, excuse me—"

"It's all right. I'll eat them both. I'm starved." He swallowed a mouthful of greenery. "Famished." He climbed up to the top of a skyscraper and peeked down at the microbes of movement thousands of miles below. He almost vomited with vertigo. Then he jumped off into space.

"What time do you finish work?" he asked her.

She just stood there.

"Waitress!" somebody yowled. "I don't have any mustard!"

"Yes, sir."

And she was gone.

The lieutenant jumped out of his chair and held up his hand like an umpire. The Eye turned. Two men and a woman were standing in the entranceway.

He spun around and looked out the window, his balls retracting as if dipped in ice water.

One of the men was Abdel Idfa. The other was—

"Hey!" somebody at the next table brayed. "Isn't that Duke Foote?"

It was Duke Foote indeed! Who else could it have been? He was wearing gazelle trousers, a Buffalo Bill jacket, snake boots, and a John Wayne hat. "Howdy!" he yodeled. And he and Abdel escorted the woman to the lieutenant's table.

She was in a very simple RAF blue woolen dress and matching headband and carried a bag of striped hemp. A silver zodiacal disc hung from her neck.

She was Dr. Martine Darras from Boston.

＊　＊　＊

The Eye watched them frozen with dismay. He refused to believe that this was really happening. It was too stark. No disaster could be so colossal.

Now they were shaking hands with the lieutenant, sitting down like old friends. Behind them, covering the entire wall from floor to ceiling, was a bright mural depicting George Washington crossing the Delaware in a fleet of longboats filled with ragged continental riflemen. The soldiers enclosed the table, rising among the four of them like a ballet of invalid madmen.

"Duke Foote?" someone was asking. "Didn't he marry Michelle Phillips?"

"No," somebody else piped up. "You're thinking of Dennis Hopper."

"Well, wasn't he with the Mamas and Papas?"

"Dennis Hopper?"

"No, Duke Foote!"

"Nah, Duke's a folker."

Joanna came out of the kitchen carrying a tray of ice cream dishes. The Eye cringed. *Don't drop anything, Joanna . . .* please *don't make any noise . . . please!*

She didn't, but another passing waitress dropped a metal tureen and it bounced on the floor, an echoing gong of pandemonium. Every head in the room turned.

Old friends? Well, shit! Maybe they were! What the fuck, maybe the whole situation was just a farcical coincidence, a crazy quilt of hazards stitched together by some turned-on seamstress of fates. Yeah, why not? They'd all gone to Princeton together and met once a year in Trenton for an alumni dinner . . . or maybe Dr. Darras was Duke's shrink and Abdel Idfa, the Arab prick, was her boyfriend, and they were in town tonight for one of Duke's CW concerts . . . and Duke was the lieutenant's nephew or the lieutenant was Martine's uncle or something . . . and Abdel was going into the record business and had contacted Duke to cut some albums for him, and they were all just having a bite to eat together before the show . . .

Oh, God. He almost relaxed, the full horror of the disaster anesthetizing him. No, Jesus! It was an FBI setup all the way. A Fed would come out of the woodwork now, and the five of them would—Yeah! There he was, pushing

through the crowd—the same shabby little motherfucker
he'd had lunch with! There he was! He was shaved now
and wearing a clean shirt, but he still looked grubby and
unwashed.

Okay. This was it. Wow!

Washington was across the fucking Delaware! The Hes-
sians were surrounded!

Duke was here to identify Nita Iqutos from Nashville.
And Abdel Idfa, the goddamned toad, could identify Dorothea Bishop from Chicago. And Martine could identify
Joanna Eris from the White Plains concentration camp. In
fact, by Christ, she could identify *him*, too! All she had to
do was look in his direction and—

Joanna was standing before him. "I'm off at nine
thirty." She set his dessert in the middle of the salad leaves.

He glanced at his watch. It was only eight thirty! "Can't
you leave now?" he asked.

"Darling!" a woman at the next table whined. "You have
got to be kidding, doll! Where're my clams?"

"Miss, don't you have any influence at all in the
kitchen?" someone else japed.

"Wait for me outside," Joanna murmured. And she
rushed away.

A whole fucking hour to go!

The Eye watched the quintet on the far side of the room.
They hadn't seen her. Or him. The place was too crowded,
and they were in the wrong corner. Martine was lighting a
cigarette. Duke was autographing menus. The lieutenant
munched a steak. Abdel and J. Edgar Hoover were drinking screwdrivers.

He was just one night too late. It was infuriating! Yesterday would have been perfect! Perfect! The ball-breaking
capriciousness and inconsistency of fortune outraged him.
Fuck all!

Eight forty.

It was true, there were winning streaks and there were
losing streaks, and when the jinx freaked you there just
wasn't anything you could do about it. Or was there?

He considered a number of desperate ways of breaking
this shitty deadlock. He saw a fuse box over there in a
corner by the john. Maybe he could kill all the lights, then

go into the kitchen and smuggle her out the back door . . .
Yeah—then what? Or he could come up shooting with his
.45, firing blanks at the crowd. That would send these ass-
holes stampeding like steers in all directions, and he could
grab her and make a run for it . . . But run where?

The lieutenant and that little Fed fink would have Trenton boxed up within ten minutes.

He needed at least three hours . . . two hours . . . all
right, *one* hour to get her away from here and out of town.
And furthermore, he had to take a leak first!

"That's her," the Fed whispered.

Martine looked across the room. "Where?"

"Over there by the kitchen."

"What in the world is a Yankee Doodle French Fish
Course?" Abdel Idfa asked.

The Eye got up and started for the men's room. The
hostess intercepted him. "Are you leaving, sir?"

"No, I'm just—"

"We're absolutely jammed tonight! It's awful! There just
aren't any tables available! I've never seen anything like
this!"

"Neither have I."

He got as far as the fuse box, then changed his mind.
Fuck it! He came back to the table and sat down, every
nerve in his body clanging. It was ten to nine!

"That's not Joanna Eris!"

"Please keep your voice down, Doctor." The Fed turned
to the lieutenant. "Do you have somebody watching her
house?"

The lieutenant nodded, chewing a piece of pie.

"I tell you it's not her," Martine insisted.

"We have reason to believe it is, Dr. Darras."

"Which one is she supposed to be?" Duke popped out of
his chair and looked around.

"Sit down, Mr. Foote. I'll point her out to you later."

"As I told you before," Abdel Idfa nibbled a *sole aux
raisins à la Thomas Jefferson*. "I just cannot assure you
categorically that I am capable of recognizing the woman
after all this time."

"We realize that, sir. We just want you to have a look at her."

"Well, I'll sure as hell be able to recognize ol' Nita." Duke sawed a slab of roast. "Just drag her over here."

"Are you sure I'm watching the right girl?" Martine asked. "That one wearing glasses?"

"Yes."

"It isn't Joanna." She shook her head. "No."

"Which?" Duke turned. "Whereabouts? Who?"

"By the door there."

"*Her?*" Duke hooted. "You fellers bird-turdin' me or what? That there ain't Nita!"

"Knock it off, Duke," the lieutenant growled. "Stop hollering."

"Turn around, Mr. Foote," the Fed muttered. "Don't stare at her."

"I cannot see her from here." Abdel dabbed his lips with a napkin. "Can we have some more wine?"

Then Martine looked through the crowd and saw the Eye.

Nine five.

He fumbled with the *Trenton Times*, ripping it open clumsily, almost tearing it apart. He read Joanna's horoscope.

> Take advantage of this
> period of bliss and plenitude.
> You're one of the fortunate
> people who can do no wrong.
> Everything you touch today
> will turn to gold.

Gold! He was giggling. *Gold!* Giggling like an idiot! The diners at the adjacent tables smiled at him. He swallowed, almost choking on the thick bile filling his mouth. Christ, he was going to puke! No he wasn't . . . no . . . no . . . Hold tight. Nope! Cool! Why spoil everybody's meal? Unwind your abdomen! Stay insensible . . . comatose . . . numb . . .

He lowered the paper, his eyes sweeping across the room to meet Martine's gaze.

They glowered at each other.

Great! She'd spotted him! Bliss and plenitude!

Joanna passed, serving the next table. A man handed her a menu. "Would you ask Mr. Foote to sign this?" He slipped her a quarter.

"What?" She stared at him blankly.

"Duke Foote over there," he pointed. "Get his autograph for me."

"Duke Foote?" she looked dazed.

The Eye pulled out a handkerchief, wiped his streaming face. An autograph! That did it! This was the Apocalypse! The gas chamber, the firing squad, the electric chair, ruin, total havoc . . . He looked up.

The hostess was hovering over him.

"You're all alone!" she snapped at him accusingly. "Would you mind . . . ?"

"I beg your pardon . . ."

"Your table . . ."

"My table?"

"Could you share it please?" She beckoned, yelped. "Over here, you newlyweds!" A boy and a girl, crimson with embarrassment, sat down before him.

"Thanks," the boy smiled shyly.

"I'll be—be—" The Eye tried to rally what was left of his sanity. "—Be leaving in just a minute . . ."

"No rush," the boy said. He held the girl's hand. She touched his face, grinning, shining, in a coma of happiness. "Gosh," she whispered. "I could eat a horse!"

At least a hundred people waited behind the ropes now and the hostess flew around the tables, devastated. She pounced on Joanna, standing there, still holding the menu, peering around myopically.

"What are you doing, girl?" she hissed.

"Gentleman wants an autograph . . ."

"I'll get it." She snatched it away from her.

Nine ten.

"What time does she get off work, Lieutenant?" the Fed asked.

"Nine thirty. She's looking over here. I think she's on to us."

"It doesn't matter."

Martine turned to him. "You asked me to cooperate with you. All right, I've cooperated. It isn't Joanna Eris. You can take that as a formal statement. Now I want to go back to Boston."

"In due time, Dr. Darras."

"I want you to know that I find this whole business sickening. Altogether sickening."

"Would you care for a dessert?"

"I would." Abdel Idfa finished his sole. "I think I'll try some of this Bill of Rights Fudge Sundae."

"Y'know—" Duke started to say. The hostess handed him the menu. He scribbled his name on it.

"Thank you, Mr. Foote!" she cried.

"Not at all, Ma'am. The pleasure's all mine." He grabbed her hand and kissed it. She crowed with delight and soared back across the room. "Y'know," he mused, "if it is ol' Nita . . . I'm not sayin' it is or it isn't, formal and positive, mind, not like the doc here . . . but if it is her, I'm kinda lookin' forward to meetin' her again. She was a nifty little ol' girl."

"I think you'll meet her again, Mr. Foote," the Fed said.

Martine leaned back in her chair, holding her Virgo disc, squeezing it tightly.

The Eye studied the newlyweds. They were in their twenties, fresh and clean, unscarred, untarnished, as yet uncontaminated. God Almighty! Which one would betray the other first? Would they have a daughter? What cornucopia of anguish and woe and loneliness and repulsion had they been given as a wedding present by the hymeneal pixies?

It was nine twenty.

"We won't bust her here," the Fed whispered to the lieutenant. "It would only cause a fuss. We'll wait till she gets outside. Or better still, back to her place."

"Right."

"I remember just one thing about Dorothea Bishop," Abdel Idfa told them. "When Mr. Argyle introduced us, in Chicago, I asked her if she was a virgin. And she said—" He turned to Martine. "Excuse me, Doctor—she said, 'That's none of your fucking business.'"

The boy said something. The Eye turned to him. "Sorry . . ."

"You're eating my radishes."

"Your what? I am? My apologies. I . . . I'm a nervous wreck . . ."

"Be my guest."

"My daughter . . . my daughter ran away and I can't find her." He gaped at them. Why had he said that? Shit and corruption!

"Hell," the boy said.

"Is she in Trenton?" the girl asked.

"I don't know." He smiled sillily, his fingers scratching the tablecloth. "She could be. She could be anywhere. Anywhere at all. There are so many places to hide. So many back streets and lanes and suburbs and little towns and crossroads . . . and locked doors . . . and . . . and freeways going everywhere—" His voice cracked.

"The last I heard from her, she was—she was in school and she just—" Jesus Christ! He was crying! Holy Moses! He was coming apart! Ape shit! This was the fucking end! "What time is it?" he blubbered.

"Nine thirty." The boy looked desolate. "But I think my watch is slow."

"Good—yeah—okay—" the Eye gibbered. "With a little bit of luck, maybe we'll make it. Listen—" They stared at him. "I wish you all the happiness in the world. I mean that from the bottom of my heart. Let me bear all your sorrows—give me your grief and your loss. I'll take them with me now and you two just keep the joys and blessings of life. So long."

He got up and fled.

Eighteen

She was waiting for him in the parking lot. She had removed her awful Hessian disguise and was wearing a raincoat over a skirt and sweater. It was the same sweater she'd bought in Philadelphia.

"They wanted me to stay another hour." She pulled off her glasses and put them into her purse. "I told them I had to meet my brother."

"It's never been this crowded before." He led her over to the Porsche. "What's the occasion?"

"It's D-Day. There's going to be a big thing at the War Memorial Building tonight."

They drove up West State. He could feel her warmth burning beside him. He forced himself not to think of her presence. He was afraid he might crack up again. "Duke Foote was there having dinner," he said. "Did you see him?"

"Yes." She stiffened. "I saw him."

He felt a tremor run through her body. Fine! She was still reacting, anyway. Maybe her survival instincts weren't as low as he thought. "He was with those cops."

"What cops?"

"The lieutenant or whatever he is. And the other one."

They were on East State now, but heading in the wrong direction.

"Where would you like to go? How about a drink?"

"I could use a drink all right. Cops, you say? In the restaurant?"

"Yes. I pointed them out to you."

"You did?"

Good! She was really coming out of it now. Her fright was palpable. Alarms were ringing.

"I'm a stranger here. Do you know any quiet bars anywhere?" The words shocked him. He loathed the role he had to play and the dialogue he would be forced to speak for the rest of the evening.

"Please, no bars. I look too ghastly."

"My place, then?"

"Sure."

He turned north and drove up the river toward Washington's Crossing.

He wondered if she hated him.

He pulled into the motel yard and parked beside the Chevette.

It won't work, he told himself. They walked to the unit, two basket cases playing in a bumpkin production of *Samson et Dalila*, a wheezing, bald tenor and a colorless mezzosoprano smelling faintly of kitchen grease.

He unlocked the door, and they went inside. He turned on the lights, set the attaché case and the Porsche's keys on the table.

"I think they have the place staked out," he said.

"Who?" She took off her raincoat. There was a hole in the sweater's elbow.

"The cops. The restaurant. Probably going to arrest somebody."

"Who?"

"One of the customers who eats there regularly, I suppose. Or somebody who works there." He took a bottle of Martell from his valise. "Or maybe they just like the food."

She sat down and crossed her legs. There was a run in her stocking. She saw it, tried to conceal it.

He uncorked the bottle, took two ponies from the bureau, moved back and forth around the room so he wouldn't have to look at her.

"This is all I have. Do you like cognac?"

"Cognac? I never tried it."

Excellent! He poured two drinks.

"I've seen you somewhere before," she said suddenly.

His knees gave way beneath him, and he sat down on the edge of the bed. "You have? I thought you never noticed me. I've been in that place every day now for the last—"

"No. Somewhere else. Have you ever been—?" She sipped her drink, frowning. "Have you ever been to Florida?"

"Yeah. A couple of times."

She shrugged. "Everybody looks familiar. This is very good." She took another sip. "Have you ever been to LA?"

"No."

"What are you doing in Trenton?"

"Just driving through. And you?"

"I was born here." She got up. "I'm filthy. Could I use your shower?"

"Go ahead."

She carried her glass into the bathroom. The .45 was there, in its holster, hanging on the back of the door.

He opened her purse. It contained her glasses, a dirty handkerchief, a felt pen, her battered *Hamlet* paperback, and several wrapped cubes of sugar marked The Hessian Barracks.

She leaned out of the bathroom, nude. "By the way, my name is Rita Holden."

"Glad to know you, Rita." He pushed the purse behind him.

"Who are you?"

"Me? Oh—nobody in particular. I'm an accountant."

"Can I have another?" She handed him her empty pony.

He took the bottle from the table, walked over to her. She covered her breasts coyly.

"You don't want to talk about yourself?"

"Not really." He poured her a double shot.

"What about me? Shall I tell you the story of my life?"

"Certainly."

He sat down on the bed again. They would be safe here for a little while. And if she drove all night she could lose them by tomorrow. They'd close in on her again sooner or later, but she could have weeks—months—maybe even a year of reprieve.

She turned on the shower. "My father was a famous shoplifter," she called. "Interpol and Scotland Yard and the FBI chased him for years and years. But they could never catch him. He was too cunning. Then one night— Can you hear me?"

"Yes." He put his face in his hands. *Rita*. Where had he heard that name before?

"Then one Christmas he dropped dead in a department store, his pockets filled with stolen jewelry. That's how they caught him. Finally. But it was too late. He just died. It was Christmas. He had the last word. 'Merry Christmas,' he said. And he passed away, cheating them of their punishment."

Christmas Eve, yes. Saint Rita! In that church in Baltimore. *O lovely saint*, he prayed, *let her kill me and be at peace for a while!*

"That's not true," she laughed. "He was a doctor. A well-known gynecologist. He was struck by lightning one night while delivering a baby in a stable in Bethlehem, Pennsylvania." She laughed again, turned off the shower and began whistling "La Paloma."

He opened the attaché case, took out the money, counted the fifties: one, two, three, four, five, six . . . Would she stay naked and continue to play this sad game with him? Eleven, twelve, thirteen, fourteen, fifteen . . . If he only knew where Maggie was, he'd give her a thousand dollars, too. It must be pleasant to be able to do that, he thought . . . give your daughter presents and money . . .

She came out of the bathroom. She was dressed, holding the .45. "Look what I found," she said.

"Be careful." He got to his feet. "It's loaded." He put the bills back into the attaché case. "Don't worry, I'm not a mobster or anything like that. I have a permit for it. I usually carry a lot of money around with me."

"How much do you have there?"

"Quite a bit."

She shot him, twice. He spun back across the room, slamming into the bureau, then to the floor.

She threw the gun aside, pulled on her raincoat. She picked up the attaché case and the Porsche's keys and ran outside.

He heard her drive away. Hallelujah!

He pulled himself up and leaned against the table. She'd

forgotten her purse. And her glasses. He took them, closed
his valise, corked the bottle of Martell, picked up the .45,
carried everything out to the yard and threw them into the
Chevette.

He drove out to the Turnpike and followed her.

Off and away!

He hoped she didn't intend to go back to Yard Avenue.
They would be watching the rooming house.

She didn't. She drove through Mercerville, passing the
Mercer County Home for Girls. She probably didn't even
see it. What could she see without her glasses? Avalanches
of light, a blizzard of colors.

She was going too fast.

She soared through Hightstown, then Princeton. Now
she was in a long dark tunnel of trees on the bank of a
river. Where was she going? Was she wearing her belt? A
truck rolled out of a driveway in front of her. It swerved
wildly to avoid the Porsche, its brakes squeaking. It banged
into a parapet. Baskets tumbled to the road. The Eye
passed, driving through a million bouncing apples.

She swooped into Pennington, missed a turn in the
street, and cut across the corner of a lawn, smashing over a
swing and demolishing a garden table. A crowd of people
on the house's front porch came shrieking toward her. She
sledded along a pavement to the street, sideswiping a
parked car.

She drove through the town like a hurricane, up one avenue and down another, looking for an exit. Then she burst
out into the Ewing road, just missing a passing taxi. Their
two fenders touched and grated.

Come on, Joanna, stop it!

She veered suddenly and skidded into a siding. She hit
the brakes, sailed into a plowed field. She backed quickly
out to the highway, slamming against a post.

*Don't panic! Park somewhere and wait until it's day-
light!*

At the next intersection she scraped a roadsign. She
zoomed through Ewing at eighty miles per hour. She
braked again for no visible reason and hurtled into a pile of
cans stacked on a curb, sending them clanging all over the
roadway.

Why are you going so fucking fast?

She roared through Mercerville again, repassed the girls' home. She'd fled in an immense circle and now was back on the Hightstown road.

It began to rain.

Just keep moving, Flatfleet always said, *and they'll never catch you.*

Well, they'd certainly kept moving. Godalmighty, how they had moved! It had been a long, long travelogue, indeed!

And they'd never been caught.

But it was all over now. This was their last road. He knew that the instant he saw her wheels lock.

The Porsche slid sideways into a fence, pulverized it, and flew into a billboard.

No more motels. No more cars. No more money. No more airports.

He waited for the flames.

No more wigs. No more pears. No more horoscopes.

He stopped, opened the door, jumped out to the grass. No flames. The horn was blaring like a trumpet, but it wasn't burning. He raced through the breached fence, fell down a slope, jumped around the billboard. It wasn't burning.

No more cognac. No more Gitanes. No more sharks and rattlesnakes.

She was hanging out the window, upside down, the rain slashing her face.

He took her by the shoulders, pulled her to the ground, lifted her, carried her up the slope. It still wasn't burning. He stumbled across the highway, laid her out on a knoll of weeds.

He remembered her in her bookstore on Hope Street. He remembered her standing with her hands on her hips in New York and Chicago and Nashville.

Her nose was broken. Her ears were bleeding.

He remembered her skiing in Sun Valley and swimming in the Mississippi at dawn.

Her eyes opened, and she smiled at him. "Yes, I know you," she said. "You were in the park . . . you had a camera . . . you took my picture . . ."

And the Porsche exploded, throwing sunflowers of fire over their heads.

He looked across the road at the billboard and finally solved Crossword Puzzle Number Seven.

DRINK PILSEN—THE
CZECHOSLOVAKIAN BEER!

The flames whipped it, swallowing all the letters except OSLO, a capital in Czechoslovakia.

Nineteen

Shakespeare and *The Decline and Fall of the Roman Empire* and most of the thick new books tired his eyes. But he had no trouble at all reading Zane Grey, Max Brand, Edgar Rice Burroughs, Sax Rohmer, Rex Stout, Erle Stanley Gardner, or Ellery Queen. He went through everything they ever wrote.

But he spent most of his time building model airplanes. His specialty was World War II fighters. He had whole squadrons of Stukas, Thunderbolts, ME 109s, FW 190s, Spitfires, Mustangs, and Zeros lined up on shelves all over the cottage.

In the mornings he'd go for walks in the hills or drive to Fresno to do his shopping.

The cottage was only a few miles from the San Joaquin River and in the afternoons he would go to the cemetery to visit Joanna.

Her real name was engraved on her headstone

JOANNA ERIS

with the dates of her birth and death. Her epitaph was

Rest, perturbed spirit.

That had been one of the many passages underlined in her paperback *Hamlet*. He'd chosen it at random.

He would sit beside her grave for hours, chatting with her, sharing their memories, telling her stories.

When are you coming to bed? she would ask. And they would both laugh. This was their daily joke. It referred to the nearby burial plot he'd bought for himself. It was all ready for him.

At sunset he would go home.

He'd watch television in the evening, then read or work on his planes until midnight, then either lie on his cot or sit in his armchair and doze until dawn.

After her accident, when he'd had her body flown to California, the FBI had pulled him in for questioning several times.

They wanted to know who and what he was and why he was so interested in the "subject" Rita Holden AKA Nita Iqutos, AKA Charlotte Vincent AKA Dorothea Bishop, etc., etc., née Joanna Eris.

He'd told them vaguely about his involvement in the Paul Hugo case when he was working for Watchmen, Inc. (He'd felt that this was somehow fitting, ending her story as it began, with Paul Hugo. It more or less closed the circle.) He hadn't given them any details. He'd merely stated that during the course of a routine inquiry—years ago!—he'd encountered the "subject" in Chicago . . . or had it been San Francisco? Or LA? Anyway, he'd met her again in Trenton when she was working as a waitress in The Hessian Barracks. He'd invited her out to dinner. They'd had a few drinks together, then she'd stolen his Porsche. He'd claimed her body because he'd wanted her to have "a Christian burial."

They'd only half believed him.

They'd put him in a lineup and brought in Duke, Abdel Idfa, and Martine to see if they could identify him. Duke and Abdel hadn't the faintest idea who he was, and Martine had played dumb.

Later she and the Eye had had a few seconds alone together in the outer office. They hadn't spoken. They'd both been afraid of bugs, so they just stood there staring at each other gravely. Then the Feds had called her into the other room, and before leaving she'd winked at him.

He laughed, remembering it. A wink was as good as a nod!

Finally, after the third or fourth interrogation, he'd told them all to go fuck themselves. They hadn't retaliated.

And he'd gone to Fresno and rented his cottage—his "antechamber" as Joanna called it. *Hurry up!* she kept saying. *It's cold in here alone!*

His neighbors thought he was a widower. The kids called him Pop. His landlady, a swinging young matron who lived in Reedly, adored him. "Did you see what he's done to that hovel!" she would rave to her friends. "The roof and the windows and the porch? It looks brand new! Why, even the john works! If he wasn't such an old dear I'd kick his ass out of there and sell the place for eighty thousand dollars!"

And time passed. Midnight, dawn, the morning, the afternoon, and twilight.

Once every five or six months he'd clean his .45 and drive to Oakland or San Mateo and hold up somebody for a few hundred dollars. This kept him in spending money and paid his rent. Only occasionally would he ask himself, *What the fuck am I doing?* The answer was always the same: *Waiting.*

Every so often he'd spend an evening with Father Anthony, the local priest. They'd drink beer and play gin and talk about football and God.

"The Oakland Raiders, that was the team! Remember Cozie? And remember Ken Huff of the Colts?"

"Mike Fanning was probably the best."

"Fanning couldn't come anywhere near Cozie or Ken Huff. But my all-time favorite was Bartkowski!"

"He played with the Eagles, didn't he?"

"What are you saying? The Eagles! He was with the Falcons. . . . Uhh . . . was that little girl down in the cemetery baptized?"

"No, Father."

"And if I—uhh—read the names on the stones correctly, she was born out of wedlock?"

"Yes, Father."

"Well—uhh—of course Fanning was great too. The last time I saw the Rams play was in seventy-five. Live, I mean. Against the Forty-niners. . . ."

"What does God see, Father, when he looks at us?"

The question didn't take the priest aback. He was a wise old man who had served in many parishes, and nothing surprised him. "If I knew that, pal," he laughed, "I'd be God myself. Whatsoever he beholdeth is for his eyes only."

On the last night of his life the Eye dreamed of the corridor. He found the door, and it was unlocked. He opened it and stepped into the photograph.

And there he was!

The fifteen lovely faces turned to him, alive and miraculous and startled.

He stood before them, absolutely certain that he was awake and that everything else, the whole long, long saga of his longing, had been a dream.

Maggie? he asked.

But he died before his lost daughter could answer him. And they buried him beneath the oak trees beside his inviolate bride.

LOVE IS A RACKET

BY JOHN RIDLEY

Jeffty Kittridge, ex–wannabe scriptwriter and small-time Hollywood con, is deep in debt to a ruthless shark with a need to collect. What Jeffty needs is salvation. A plan. A partner. He's got all three in Mona. Street-hard and angel-beautiful, she's got one last chance for the big time, too.

Together they're going to make a killing in the ultimate scam. But where it leads them is as dark as night—a common ground where passion has a body count, trust explodes at point-blank range, and the biggest racket in town is the easiest one to fall for.

Published by Ballantine Books.
Available in bookstores everywhere.

CRAZY IN ALABAMA

by Mark Childress

Meet Peter Joseph, aka Peejoe, a wide-eyed believer in the unbelievable, raised by his Meemaw in Pigeon Creek for a good part of his life. But it was his aunt Lucille who raised him for the better. And it all happened during that summer everyone was driven crazy in Alabama, with Lucille at the wheel.

How do you become a movie star when you're on the run for murder? Lucille's got a plan. Not to mention a tank full of gas, a hopped-up sense of liberty, and her number one fan, Peejoe, by her side. It was a darn good week for Lucille. But for Peejoe, it would be the journey of a lifetime. . . .

*Now a major motion picture
starring Harrison Ford and
Kristin Scott Thomas!*

RANDOM HEARTS
by Warren Adler

He's a happily married man. She's a happily married woman, with a daughter and a dog. There's absolutely no reason why they should ever meet.

Until a commercial airliner crashes into the Potomac River. Two of the victims are linked by a clue that at first stuns and baffles, then draws together their surviving spouses.

The explosive discovery leads them on a journey that forces them to confront the mysterious and random nature of love—and the transforming power it wields over men and women caught in its relentless maelstrom.

Published by Ballantine Books.
Available in bookstores everywhere.

*Now a major motion picture
starring Meg Ryan, Diane Keaton,
and Lisa Kudrow!*

HANGING UP
by Delia Ephron

"Wonderful . . . Eve Mozell is having a lousy day, and she hasn't even gotten past breakfast yet. Her father, a senile ex-alcoholic whose idea of a good joke is goosing his woman doctor, started phoning Eve at 6 a.m. Her teenage son, who alternately ignores and lectures her, is off to a séance. ('You know, Mom, all doors are entrances. Think about it.') And a quick glance in the mirror turns out to be a big mistake. 'Oh God, is that my face? . . . I need a vacation. No. This is just me. Me at forty-four.' . . . What a terrific debut."
—*Newsweek*

"Hilarious . . . A charming, entertaining read."
—*Los Angeles Times*

Published by Ballantine Books.
Available in bookstores everywhere.